CITY OF NOTIONS

THE SHADOW OVER PORTSMOUTH BOOK 3

JEFF DECK

ALSO BY JEFF DECK

City of Ports: The Shadow Over Portsmouth Book 1
City of Games: The Shadow Over Portsmouth Book 2

The Pseudo-Chronicles of Mark Huntley

Player Choice

The Great Typo Hunt:
Two Friends Changing the World, One Correction at a Time
(with Benjamin D. Herson)

Short stories featured in:

Murder Ink 2: Sixteen More Tales of New England Newsroom Crime
(Plaidswede Publishing)

Corporate Cthulhu (Pickman's Press)

Robots & Artificial Intelligence Short Stories (Flame Tree Publishing)

CITY OF NOTIONS

THE SHADOW OVER PORTSMOUTH BOOK 3

JEFF DECK

City of Notions: The Shadow Over Portsmouth Book 3
by Jeff Deck

Edition 1.0. Copyright © 2019 Jeff Deck. All rights reserved.

This story is a work of fiction. Names, characters, places, and incidents either are the product of the author's imagination or are used fictitiously. Any resemblance to actual people, living or dead, businesses, companies, events, or locales is coincidental.

Book cover design provided by Damonza.

You'll receive *Tales of the Shadow Over Portsmouth,* a FREE companion book to this series, just for signing up for my e-mail updates. Go to: www.jeffdeck.com

Thank you so much for supporting this work.

Printed in the United States of America.

❦ Created with Vellum

For Kerry, Abree, Kali, and Kate

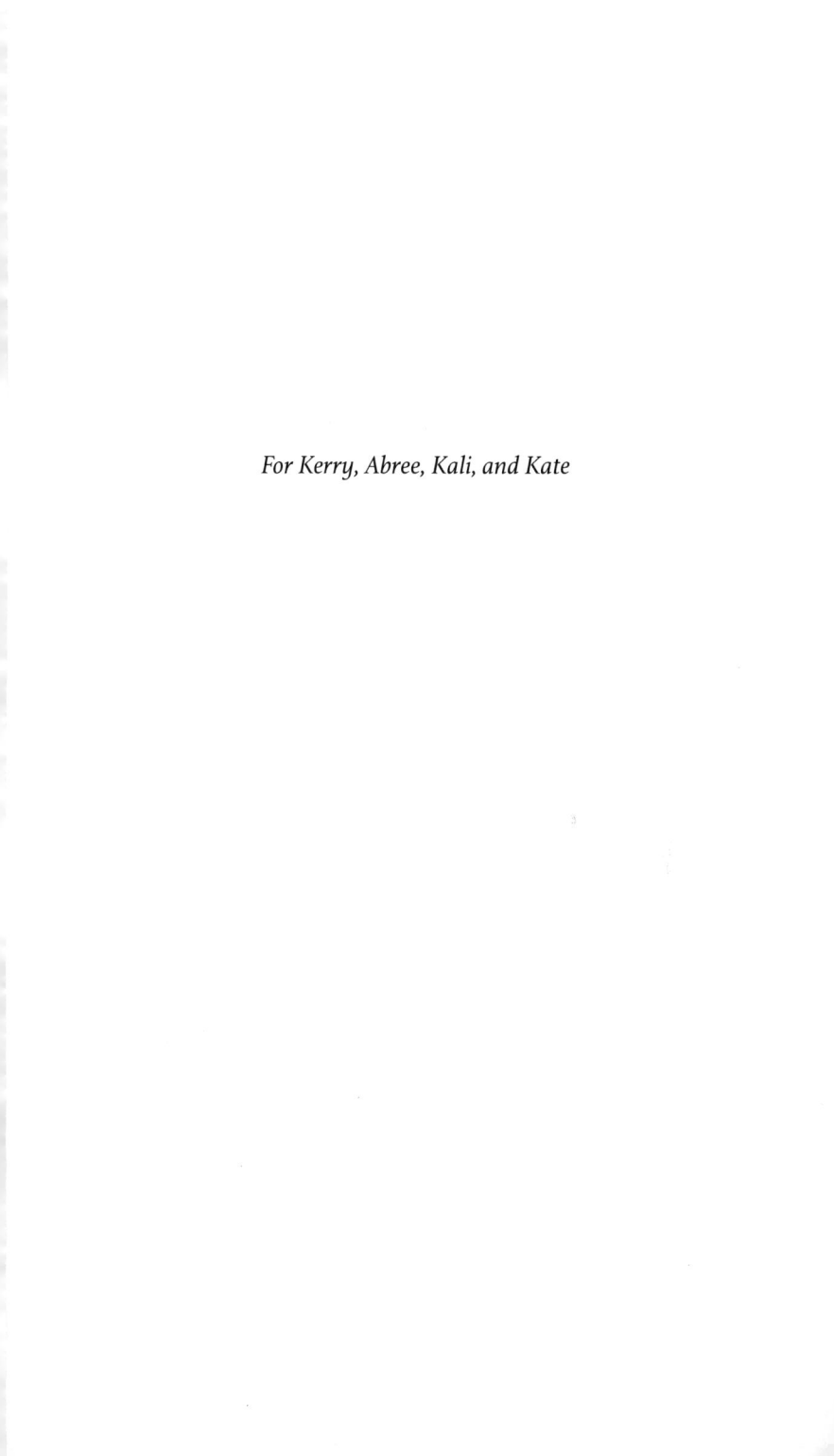

"**City of Notions.** Boston, Mass., the metropolis of New England, which is the home of 'notions,' that is, articles of all kinds, trifling in size and value, but for which there is a large sale."
— *The New People's Cyclopedia of Universal Knowledge* (1887)

"Boston is, say what you will of it, the city of 'notions,' and of new notions too; and in the progress of liberal ideas in this country, it ever has and will ever take the lead."
— Orestes Augustus Brownson, editor, *The Boston Quarterly Review* (Vol. I, 1838)

A NOTE FROM THE AUTHOR

A *Dramatis Personae* (cast of characters) for the series is now available at the end of the book. Readers that get confused about names and places while going through this story are invited to flip ahead and consult the Dramatis Personae, which contains few spoilers about this book (but many about the previous books).

— JMD

1

I'm sitting across from Special Agent Jeong in the dim Portsmouth Book and Bar, drinking an espresso and restraining myself from driving down to Boston *right now*.

It's approaching eleven p.m. Sara, the server behind the bar, gives Jeong and me the eye. She must be wondering how long us two barnacles will stick to the hull of the place. I didn't expect my evening to turn out like this. Until Jeong called, I intended to relax at my place and recover from The Kiss that Nadia Chopin planted on me in Stroyer's Axle. Now my confused emotions have retreated to a far corner of my heart, replaced by a more familiar beat for the bitter old organ: Anger.

"You *promised* me Benazir would be safe," I say.

Ethan Jeong looks more lined in the face than when I last saw him. Handsome guy, but his smile hasn't been so quick since he suffered repeated mind control out on Round Island (and beyond), that brutal day a few weeks ago. He can't look at me with the same frankness as before, either, given that he nearly beat me to death in the palace of another world. My fractured cheek still remembers, too.

"I shouldn't have," he says. "But now that I do know better, I've come to you right away with my new intel. They're going to open Benazir up as soon as tomorrow." He pauses. "I don't want you to do anything crazy."

"Ethan, if you *really* wanted that, you wouldn't have told me they're going to torture Benazir," I say.

He spreads his hands. "Okay. Maybe there's an element of passing the buck. What I want is for you not to do anything crazy on your own."

"But you've already said there's nothing you can do."

"There's nothing I can do *officially*," Jeong says. "Unofficially, I'll support you however I can. I'm—I'm responsible for this, and I intend to take responsibility."

We're the only customers left in the Book and Bar. The rest of the Friday night crowd has moved on to other venues (down on Daniel Street there's even a bar open until 1 a.m., here in the City That Often Sleeps!). I doubt sour Sara is a creature of the city council, so we're safe to speak freely. "So tell me," I say. "The layout of the Boston office. The security in the area where they're keeping Benazir. How many times am I gonna get shot before I reach her?"

"Too many," Jeong says. "Highly trained federal agents are there to make sure you don't reach the classified containment area in the basement. The cell itself will have a biplanar lock similar to the ones we've got in the McIntyre Building here in town. And I guarantee you my keys won't work on the locks down in Boston, even if I finagled my way to the cells themselves."

Thanks to the espresso, my mind is getting in gear again, whirling around the information Jeong has shared. Something about the freaky lock—a thought itches at the back of my mind. It feels familiar, as if I've wondered the same about the biplanar locks at Jeong's office.

"So is there a possibility," I ask, "that you could get to the cell? Even if you don't have the authority to free her?"

"I'd have to have a damned good reason," Jeong says.

"But it's not impossible," I press.

He frowns. "I suppose not. What good would it be, though, if I can't get her out of the cell?"

Maybe he can, halfway. "Tell me more about the biplanar locks," I say. "What plane, exactly, are they poking into?"

Sara at the counter says, "Hey, guys. You mind cashing out?"

"One sec," I say, holding up a finger. Jeong is deep in thought.

Finally he says, "For the ones in my office, a guy from Boston set them up. I didn't have the authority to ask questions about the workings of the lock. Probably still don't."

"The locks in your office. Do they involve the *same* dimension or world as the locks in Boston?" I ask.

Sara flips off half the lights in the Book and Bar. I miss Val, the pugnacious, curly-haired girl who used to work here. She'd never have pulled this passive-aggressive shit. But Val went missing a long time ago, just another person this hungry city swallowed and digested. I'd suspect the city council if not for the fact that Councilor Wegman is Val's father.

I stalk over to Sara and lay down a wad of cash. It represents the last of my checking account. "Can this buy us an extra ten minutes, *please*?" I ask her.

But Jeong says, "No, let's go."

He stands up and shrugs on his coat, though he doesn't need it for the warm night. "Come on, Ethan—" I say.

"We'll walk and talk," he says.

I take my cash back. (I do need it.) Jeong pauses on the sidewalk outside, but I steer him toward Daniel Street, where the FBI office awaits. I don't like the slouch in Ethan Jeong's formerly upright carriage, the grey cast to his face. I whack him on the shoulder, and he halts, surprised.

"The locks," I say. "I know you've been through a lot these past couple of months—maybe the Bureau's not what you thought it was. Maybe none of these frigging institutions are." I shudder at the memories of my past self... my past angrier self, the Ogre of Portsmouth. "I went through my own come-to-Jeebus moment not all that long ago, as you may recall. Protect and serve... fidelity, bravery, integrity... all the mottos, all the mission statements, it's all bullshit."

"This is supposed to make me feel better?" he says wryly.

"You're a good man, Ethan," I say. "You're bigger than any organization, no matter how many offices they have and how many people in the chain of command. Only you get to decide what bravery and integrity mean to *you*. Don't let all these corrupt, evil fuckers change who you are."

Jeong's brows knit. "I... never expected a pep talk from you, Divya. You're full of surprises."

He resumes walking, and as he turns the corner at the Breaking New Grounds coffeeshop, he mutters, "And you're not an entirely evil person yourself."

"Thank you, Agent," I say. "I'll put that on my website."

"The locks here in Portsmouth might tap into the same world as Boston, though it's impossible to know for sure," Jeong says, regaining clarity. "Same, uh, technician worked them both up."

"I don't suppose you could give him a call?"

"Not without rousing all sorts of suspicion."

I dig in my bag for the wrist thingy Nadia gave me. She called it a *Compass*. "I'd like to use this near the locks at your office."

Jeong looks at it curiously. "That's one of the devices the cultists have? I thought you need to implant it in your wrist."

"Apparently I can still use it in some limited fashion," I say.

"But how did you—"

"Nope," I say. "I don't kiss and tell. Will you let me try it?"

He nods. "I'm the acting SSA, even with the internal investigation, though I might not retain the title for long. Best get you in there while I can."

Before my twin-clone is tortured to death and dissected would be great, I think, but it's better not to rush the guy if I don't have to. We arrive at the ugly Brutalist bulk of the federal building.

Agent Jeong leads the way. Agent Lena Barnes is the only one in the dark, cramped office tonight; she gives us a curt greeting and then returns to her paperwork. She's hurting over the loss of her colleague, Mike McGuinness, who ate his own gun not long ago while under mind control. I remember Barnes's furious face at the funeral, seeing that McGuinness had been denied military honors due to his supposed suicide. She had seemed ready to dig up the corpse and personally drive it to Arlington National Cemetery.

I concentrate on the Compass in my hands, trying to detect a vibration, or see a light go on, or whatever. It might have shuddered for a second, but now I don't feel anything, even as we approach the holding cells. I experiment by holding it close to the strange keys in Jeong's hand, but it only shakes once and then remains still. There's no readout on it, no source of information I can see. I should have asked Nadia for an instruction manual for the damn thing.

"Well?" Jeong asks.

I'd hoped it would flash a color to show what type of Port the keys' dimension is—earth, fire, water, air, or quintessence—but nope, nothing. I guess these dimensional shards are too small for the Compass to react much in its unimplanted state.

"Nothing," I say. "I'm gonna need a real Portwalker to take a look at these locks and keys. Mind if I bring in a consultant?"

"This office isn't open for tours. I'm pushing it enough having you in here. Barnes won't hesitate to report me if I bring someone else in here tonight."

"Send her on an errand. Do what you have to do."

"Well. All right, I've got a promise to keep. But tell me you're not thinking of bringing in that head cultist, Chopin."

"Nadia helped Milly out, remember," I say. "When we brought Milly back from Avariccia, who else could we turn to? Now, thanks to Nadia, Milly could regain some form of sight someday."

"Jury's out on that," Jeong says. "But—more importantly, I don't *trust* this woman, Divya. I'm surprised you do, when her cult was the reason that..."

His mouth snaps shut, but it's too late. Nadia's cult was the reason you got killed. "Hannah was responsible for her own actions," I say. "She knew what she was getting into, and a city councilor murdered her, not Nadia. Look, I know the FBI and cults don't historically get along, but you've got to make an exception for her. For me."

Jeong presses his fingers to his lips. "You're the boss. If

you're sure you trust her... call her. I'll tell Barnes to pack it in for the night."

Nadia programmed the Compass she gave me with the ability to contact her wherever she is—whatever *world* she's in. But in this case, I'm able to reach her by phone.

She doesn't ask why I need her. She doesn't hesitate when I mention the meeting place, despite the fact that she and her people fear the Feds almost as much as the city council. She just says:

"Be there in a few."

I meet Nadia Chopin, unofficial leader of the Portwalkers, down in front of the McIntyre Building. Across the street, people are hollering and smoking and laughing outside the D Street Tavern, but the noise dims as soon as Nadia shows up.

I saw her only a few hours ago, but I feel like I'm seeing her for the first time: her dark-blonde hair framing a heart-shaped face with an impish grin, her athletic frame visible against her tight clothes (she's changed from the Stroyer's Axle outfit). Her green eyes seem to give off their own light in the darkness of the overhang at the McIntyre entrance.

I push my inconvenient feelings down, resist meeting her arms for a hug, and say, "Thanks for getting here so quickly. I know this is not a—hrm—safe space for you."

"I hope," she says, "you can trust me as much as I trust you. I trust you're not setting me up."

"Th-thank you," I say. Once again Nadia's throwing me off balance. Now that I know mind control is real, I almost suspect her to be bewitching me with those eyes, shining at me from under knitted dark brows. "It's my evil twin. Benazir. Something unspeakable will happen to her if I don't intervene."

"Heroic," Nadia says. She's not mocking me—just drawing attention to our conversation from earlier tonight, at the restaurant in Stroyer's Axle. During which she pinned me with a label I can't rightly own.

"Stop," I say. "Follow me."

We ascend to the FBI office on the third floor, Nadia sticking close behind me. I've never seen her show fear before, but she's showing it now. When her muscular arm intertwines with my own, I don't shrug it off, no matter what Lena Barnes might think when we enter together.

As it happens, Barnes only mutters, "I hope you got permission from the SSA." Pointedly avoiding Jeong's name. Maybe she blames him for McGuinness's death even more than she does me, though it's possible she hates us both.

I direct Nadia toward the cells. Agent Jeong is tapping something on his phone when we arrive; he pockets it and straightens at the sight of her.

"I don't believe we've officially met," he says. "I'm Supervisory Special Agent Ethan Jeong. I don't care—tonight—about your secretive organization. We simply need your help identifying another dimension."

"Oh, is that it?" she says dryly, but she fixes Ethan with a charming smile. "I've heard a lot about you from Divya."

She hasn't let go of me. I separate from Nadia and say to Jeong, "Don't worry, nothing but wine and roses. Now show her your keys."

Nadia rolls her sleeve up. The Compass implanted in her wrist is showing a lot more activity than my useless one did; minute vibrations shake her pale skin. There's no readout I can see, but she's already nodding, as if the Compass is speaking a language only she can hear.

Jeong gets the keys out, and Nadia's eyes widen. She

glances at the nearby locks, seeing them for the first time. "Where did you *get* this stuff?" she says.

"I'm sorry, but I can't say," Jeong replies.

Nadia's pleasant demeanor vanishes, replaced with a steely look I've seen before. "Did you kidnap a member of my—organization?" she asks with blunt force. "We've had people go missing. Thanks to Divya, we know the city council is responsible for some of them, but... tell me the truth, Agent Jeong."

"The FBI doesn't kidnap people," Jeong responds with haughty certainty. Then I can see him recalling the Bureau's recent activities. "At least, not often. To my knowledge, Ms. Chopin, the creation of these keys and locks had nothing to do with your group. My office only recently became aware that Ports exist at all."

"Then how did you *make* these things, if you didn't know about Ports?" She holds out her hand for the keys, which Jeong reluctantly surrenders. She turns them over in her palm. "And how in the *hell* do these keys maintain their connection with the other plane while moving? Every Port I've ever seen is fixed in one place."

"I don't think Ethan knows, never mind what he's at liberty to say," I say, interceding for both their sakes. "He didn't make the keys or locks himself. And we don't have time to debate how they were made—what's important is we figure out which other plane they're interacting with."

"Why?" Nadia asks.

"Because I'm *going* to that other plane," I say, voicing my plan for the first time, "and breaking some goddamn locks."

Jeong says, "Allard, hold up. Back up like a dozen steps for us tortoises in the back row, okay?"

"It's simple," I say. "You're going down to the Boston field office. I'm going down to wherever the lock crosses over in the other world. I bust the locks on my side of the universe. You pull off the lock to Benazir's cell and get her out of the building."

Jeong's eyes bug out. "That's—making a *lot* of assumptions on your part, Allard. For God's sake, I—"

"Wait, wait," Nadia says. "This is your evil twin, you said?"

I quickly explain what happened to Benazir. She nods once, twice. Then she says, "Let's at least find out where you're going to be traveling, then. If we can even get you there. Once you're there, it may not be a picnic either."

"I'm assuming it won't be, based on my experiences thus far," I say.

"I haven't vetted this plan of yours yet," Jeong protests. But he gives Nadia some space as her eyes half-lid and she places her Compass wrist against one of the door locks.

She stays still for almost a minute, the picture of utmost concentration. She mutters to herself, "Breath..."

Breath, not *breathe.* Curious. I wait for her to come back to us. When she does, I'm startled to see Nadia is smiling.

"You're in luck, Divya," she says. "Not only do I know what the other plane is, but I've *been* there. It's a world a lot like ours. Almost identical, in fact. You can rent a car and get down to the other Boston in no time... the hardest part may be figuring out how to get into *their* FBI office."

"They'll have an FBI office too?" I say, thinking it through. "Well, fuck. They've probably got the same biplanar locks, if we're *their* other plane. Making their locks just as impenetrable."

"Maybe not," Nadia says. "Not if you strike them in both worlds at the same time—that would set up a resonance to destroy them on both sides."

"Oh, sure," Jeong says. "Infiltration of two different FBI

offices simultaneously. No problem. Coordinated smashing locks at the exact same second in two worlds with no way to contact each other... null sweat, my friends."

The greyness is creeping into Jeong's face again. I can't blame him—this does sound impossible when put into, well, words.

But then Nadia speaks up: "That second part we've got covered, at least. Divya, can I temporarily take back your gift?"

"Oh," I say. I hand her the Compass—and she gives it to Jeong.

"Take good care of it," she says. "Divya'll want it back."

But... wait. "I thought that Compass could only contact you," I say.

"Right, and I'll be with you," Nadia says, smiling. "I'm coming with you. Unless you object?"

My eyes widen. It sure would be nice to have a friend along for the trip—

Friend, hmm—

But I can't ask her to help me break into a guarded federal facility? Can I?

"Are you *sure* about this?" I ask her.

"Hey, every hero needs a sidekick," Nadia purrs.

I scratch the back of my head violently. I want this, but I don't *really* want this. "Listen, it hasn't worked out so great for my last couple sidekicks," I say.

Nadia's sleeve is rolled down from exposing her Compass; she flexes her well-toned bicep now, unsubtly. "Do you know how many worlds I've visited so far, Divya?" she says. "This one will be incredibly tame, and we'll figure out the FBI part of the mission in no time. I'm going. You need my brains *and* brawn, my friend."

Jeong looks relieved to hear this. But then, remembering

his own questionable role in the "mission" ahead, his mouth tightens again. "So—where is the Port to enter this tame world? Nice and secluded, I hope, for your sake."

"Well..." Nadia says. "That might be a tiny problem in itself."

2

You loved Market Square Day in Portsmouth each summer for the sensory overload: the sweating masses of runners in the morning, the crowds shoving to examine the cheesy bits of jewelry in the vendor tents and jockeying for position in the fried dough line, the mediocre local bands pounding away on the Pleasant Street stage right outside our apartment. You were a sense junkie, I've come to realize. No wonder each new world you discovered would never be enough.

I, on the other hand, I've never been a fan of crowds. So Portsmouth's big July festival never held much appeal for me—and right now I'm cursing that the city ever started the tradition. Especially since, thanks to my redoubled power of hearing gained from that rotten Avariccian Chaum, the crowd noise is worse for me than it's ever been.

I hear everything. I. Hear. Everything.

It's Saturday morning and a bright, sunny, *hot* Market Square Day has arrived to fill merchants' pockets. People and tents jam the streets; the downtown area is closed to vehicles for the day. I smell arepas and gyros and fries.

Brightly colored balloons are tied together in rainbow-like arcs over the square. Many of my former colleagues are stationed around the festival to keep order. Above it all the white North Church spire stretches, proud and complacent as ever.

And kids are screaming. Runners are stretching and boasting. A fiddle duo is profaning a rock classic. Theo LaPlante, a nutty top-hat-wearing preacher from public-access TV, is giving an impromptu sermon. People are gabbing, people are hawking t-shirts and wooden joke signs, people are *chewing*. Unholy gods, so much chewing.

Nadia Chopin and I are pressed tightly together, giving me uncomfortable frissons of electricity, as we navigate Congress Street. I'm struggling mightily to enclose all irrelevant sounds and voices around me behind the stage curtain of my mind, but plenty are slipping underneath.

Oh, it just *had* to be daytime. Agent Ethan Jeong couldn't show up at the Boston field office in the middle of the night. That's logical, but *why* do we have to cross to another dimension during Portsmouth's busiest day of the year? In the very moments before the 10K race begins?

Here's the problem: Nadia's Port is inside the Portsmouth Athenaeum, the city's private library. The Athenaeum is here on the square at Congress Street, right where all the runners are congregating. We have to get inside without anyone noticing.

The Athenaeum is closed on Market Square Day. When we get to the door, it'll be locked.

We need to time our trip down to alternate Boston exactly with Jeong's drive down to our-world Boston. We'll only have a crude way to communicate, through the Compass he's borrowing from me that can ping Nadia's location. Once he's down in Boston, Jeong will enter the FBI field office and make his way to Benazir's cell without arousing suspicion.

We batted around versions of the game plan until the wee hours, trying to come up with a compelling story. Jeong traded texts with his man on the inside down there, Agent Jacob Harriman, the one who tipped him off about the upcoming torture and dissection. We settled on the following:

Jeong's under investigation for the Round Island debacle, and he's desperate to showcase his accomplishments—and improve them if he can. So he's going down to extract information from Benazir about World 72 (her world of origin).

This morning, Jeong made a call to the field office about his visit, to avoid suspicion. That ties Nadia and me to a specific timeframe for getting into the locked Athenaeum and going through the Port. We also have a particular time for striking the lock on the other side and setting off the resonance.

I'm vibrating with tension, trying to focus. I might have marshaled all of my attention away from the din and toward the mission. But in the press of the runners and the tourists, I collide with the one person who could push me over the edge... the Claudius to your Hamlet's ghost.

Councilor Grace Stone. She's wearing a forced smile and a festive summer outfit, making her rounds while trying on a jes' folks demeanor that fits her as well as Milly's clothes would fit me. Councilor Stone. *Your murderer.*

We come face to face. An onlooker might take us for old friends or family about to embrace, if not for the pure hatred radiating from my face and the arrogant condescension in hers. Without thinking, I grab her wrist.

"Fancy running into *you* here," I growl.

"Detective Allard," says Stone, making no attempt to escape my grasp. "How are you faring these days?"

"Hey—Divya—what are you *doing*?" Nadia says behind me. Though she must know perfectly well what I'm doing. She is, after all, the one who told me this two-faced toad killed you.

I ignore Nadia, caught up in the grip of my rage. "You must be feeling fucking footloose and f-fancy free," I say, tripping over my inadvertent tongue-twister. "You covered your tracks well—leaving no trace of your payoffs and your hit contracts at Grieg's office—but don't think I buy your innocence for a *second*."

"I'm sorry, I have no idea what you're talking about," Councilor Stone answers, maintaining her politician's awareness of the many ears around us. "But I'd be happy to discuss the matter in private sometime. Would you kindly...?"

I keep an iron grasp on the woman. Now she's looking a tad nervous, though maintaining a good smarmy face. "Great, how about right now?" I say. I move toward a nearby tent of seaside watercolors temporarily vacated by its artist, forcing Stone to come along.

"Really, Allard?" Nadia hisses in my ear. "In front of *all these people*?"

"Really," I say. Sure, my temper is riding me, but this is a rare opportunity to talk to the councilor without her retinue present. Her mistake was pretending to be a woman of the people, even for a couple of hours.

I crowd Councilor Stone into the tent, then glance over my shoulder. Nadia Chopin is gone. I can't blame her—she fears the city council above all else. They've taken so many of her fellow cultists; she could easily be next. She's already endangered herself by being seen with me.

As if reading my thoughts, Stone says calmly, "Who was that with you?"

"Nobody," I say.

"Never you mind, I'll figure it out later," she says with the same self-assurance. "But she was right—you have erred in corralling me in front of hundreds of witnesses. My little helpers are everywhere. Someone will arrive soon to persuade you away from me."

The woman's running down the clock, filibustering. "Why'd you kill Hannah?" I snarl. "How could she possibly be a threat to you and your lapdogs?"

"If I tell you I didn't kill her, you'll never believe me," Stone says. "But I'm not about to give you the 'why' for something I didn't do."

"I *know* what you councilors have been doing," I say, driven even more furious by her denial. My hand moves from her arm to her shoulder, near her scrawny neck. To her credit, she doesn't shy away as I press down on her flesh.

"Do you?"

"You forget already? The payments from that phony LLC you people set up, the payments that went to Mike Prince, the same cop who happened to handle the 'overdose' cases of Jill Haven and Eddie Barndollar. You paid Prince to, to, to grease those kids and then cover up their deaths. And you paid Gomez and Lewis to kill other Port cultists too—we'll find out who, sooner or later."

"I have no LLC."

"Goddammit, you'd better change your tune quick!"

Sure, when the Port in Prescott Park birthed Benazir, she was a creature born of my own anger. Maybe some of it drained from me in the process. And I know I've got more control over my temper than I used to. But in this instant, face to face with a brazen murderer and liar, I am *sorely* tempted to make her hurt. Badly. The Glock 26 Jeong loaned me was made for pistol whipping.

Only a small voice in my mind is holding me back, a voice that sounds like yours. *Don't. Don't. Don't.* But I know it's *not* you... in fact, I wouldn't be surprised if it's the god riding backseat passenger in my mind, mimicking you to keep me in line as it pursues its own obscure goals.

"Do you know what your city councilors do for you?" Grace Stone asks me, avoiding looking at the brown fingers gripping her pale, sun-damaged flesh. She doesn't wait for me to answer. "You are *surrounded* by prosperity in one of the wealthiest places in New Hampshire. Today, of all days, you should recognize the importance of maintaining Portsmouth's image as a desirable place to live, work, and visit. Look at all those people. Look at all those happy people."

"I don't give—"

"How do you think these tourists would react," Stone goes on, "if they knew a group of irresponsible drug addicts was going around this city opening doors to gibbering horror dimensions? Don't you think they *might be a little reluctant to visit*?" Her voice has raised a register. "Think of the jobs that would be lost, the lives that would be ruined. Everything you and I love about Portsmouth would come crashing down. Do you not understand that I am the *guardian* of this place?"

It's a relief to finally hear Stone admit knowing about the cultists. She's said nothing resembling a confession; she's too canny for that. But I can connect the dots.

"You and I don't love Portsmouth the same way," I tell her. "This is my home, but if it's maintained by murdering people, then I'd rather see it burn."

Councilor Stone quirks an eyebrow. "I won't let you burn

it down. Not any of you. I will find you all. And *you*, Detective Allard, are a nuisance I've tolerated for too long. Don't think sparing Sandy Grieg's life won you any points with me."

She adds, in a louder tone, "Now, I hope that information will satisfy you, because I *must* say hello to Mr. Derek Ham and purchase one of his wonderful paintings!"

"Oh, you're a peach, aren't you, Grace?" says an older man's tickled voice. Mr. Derek Ham, presumably the artist responsible for the bland seascapes in this tent, comes in smiling at us. His smile slips when he sees my grip on Stone's shoulder. "Is—is everything all right?"

I release her. "It's all five by five. Couldn't help but admire the fabric of our councilor's blouse. Where did you say you got it again?"

"Evolved Woman, on Market Street," says Stone evenly. "Tell them Grace sent you."

"I will, most certainly," I say, and I move away from her.

The artist fixes on me with a troubled look, as if trying to place who I am, but Stone starts cooing over his painting of the Nubble Light and his sales instincts take over. I'm forgotten, and I escape.

I wince as my head returns to turmoil, the babble rising and threatening to drown me. Stupid, stupid. I have only myself to blame for letting the noise distract me from the mission. I glance up at the clock face on the church steeple. Two minutes until nine.

Dammit. I can't miss our slim window of opportunity. I turn away from the crowd, slip behind the tents, and use the extra sidewalk space to jog down to the doorway to the Portsmouth Athenaeum. Nadia is leaning casually next to it; the look she gives me is out of sync with her posture.

"I thought you could *control* your anger now," she hisses at me.

"That was before my head cracked open for every sound within two miles to pour in," I snap back. "I don't have time to justify myself—they're lining up for the race."

Nadia shuts her mouth tight and waves at another person approaching us. Trig, the young nerd and Nadia's comrade in cultistry, isn't toting around his e-reader for once; he looks uncomfortable and pale in a Hairless Werewolves t-shirt and cargo shorts. He hails me with a muted wave and a shy smile as he says, "Divya."

I skip the greeting for our unexpected companion. "You, keep people on the street from entering or noticing. You, make sure nobody comes out of the Irish store and catches me."

Then I hustle into the small foyer containing the door to the Athenaeum. The space is shared with the door to a neighboring business, a kitschy Irish-themed vat of merchandise. It's an extremely awkward setup for breaking and entering. But it's better than if the Athenaeum entrance were right off the sidewalk. I *may* be able to get the lock off without anyone noticing. I reach into my jacket for my tools.

Trig, the designated blocker for the Irish store, crowds into the foyer. He peeks into the store and gives me an OK sign: nobody in there but a store clerk. Nadia pokes her head into the foyer as the church bongs the hour: "Stone is giving a speech. Going to be a few more minutes until the starting horn."

"You better not be planning on coming with us," I say to Trig.

"No," says Nadia, "he's here to give you a quick orientation about the nature of parallel worlds."

I rub the back of my head. It's about to throb again. "*Now?* Do—do I need this?"

"Yes," Nadia and Trig say together.

"You've walked through a couple worlds so far," Nadia says, "but none of them bore any close resemblance to ours. This one will... and it'll be easy for you to forget you're not still in *our* world. You may let your guard down."

"I thought you said the world we're headed to is a cakewalk," I say.

"Oh, it is, it is. But be ready for a certain amount of... disorientation."

"Don't mistake the other world for our world," Trig says. "Don't assume our world is the 'right' version and theirs is the 'wrong' one, or that they are somehow a derivation of us rather than a world of equal standing, with an equal timescale of billions of years originating back to the Big Bang in their own universe."

"That's under debate," Nadia puts in.

"Uh," I say.

"Technically we're just another eigenstate, not the absolute of the set or the matrix," Trig says. "Technically we should be E_1 rather than, say, E."

"What?" I ask. *Do we have to be doing this now?!*

"Basically what he means is our world is another iteration of Earth, not the 'one true Earth' or whatever," Nadia tells me. "Though I think the presence of all the Ports here would argue for our Earth to be in a position of primacy. It's, um, an ongoing point of contention."

"So when you travel to this other Earth," Trig says, "think of it, and everything in it, as E_2 rather than E_1." He pronounces them "E-two" and "E-one."

"Okay." I haven't given the semantics of alternate worlds

a second of thought before now. And now isn't the ideal time for it.

"This is *important*," he insists. "You can't think of the people over there as being the same as the ones here. Any number of factors could have influenced them to become entirely different people, even if they look the same as the ones in our eigenstate." He clears his throat, then adds with a pained expression: "Good guys could be bad guys. Do you see what I'm getting at?"

"Right. Now, Nadia, get your ass back outside and give me a signal *right* before the race begins."

She returns to the sidewalk. Trig glances back inside the Irish store—and then pales. "Oh shit. I don't know where that customer came from, but... there's a big gentleman up at the register. Getting checked out."

And he's going to walk into the foyer right as I'm busting the Athenaeum lock. Confirming my fears, Nadia pokes back in and says, "Maybe thirty seconds left."

"Occupy him," I tell Trig.

"What?"

"Occupy *the damn customer*," I snarl. "Do whatever you have to, to keep him in the store."

"But I..." Trig's look of panic is total.

I shove him through the doorway of the store. He stumbles and then, visibly trembling, approaches the "gentleman" up at the counter. "Greetings, and... top o' the morning to you, my friend..."

It's out of my hands now. I focus on the lock. Outside I hear a bellowing, microphone-amplified voice:

"Runners—listen for the air horn!"

The horn blasts seconds later. As it's sounding, I smash the lock open. I rapidly open the door, pop inside, and close the door behind me. The stairwell is quiet and dark. I ascend the first flight, ear cocked for any sounds up above me. And finally, my preternatural hearing offers me something besides a headache and temporary insanity.

I hear pages turning. A pen scribbling. Someone is in the Athenaeum. We've screwed up.

Before I can beat a retreat, the door to the foyer opens and Nadia hurries inside, closing the door behind her. "Well, *that* was close," she says in a (to my ears) incredibly carrying voice. "Trig almost got—"

Then she notices me with my index finger mashed against my lips, and she finally gets it. Good god, I would have expected more from the leader of a clandestine cult. She whispers, "What? Someone's here?"

"Yes."

"What do we do? We can't give up... what do you want to do?"

Nadia's right. Benazir doesn't have long before the Feds take their knives to her. It *has* to be today, but dammit, nobody was supposed to be working in the Athenaeum today. However, we have a chance of creeping past the "staff only" door and continuing up to the library proper if the unknown staffer didn't hear Nadia's voice in the stairwell.

The pen is still scratching.

"Let's go," I murmur. The two of us climb the stairs to the top floor and enter the library.

I don't remember how much it costs people to become a member of the Portsmouth Athenaeum, but it's some crazy amount per year. As I recall, it's limited to only a few hundred members at a time. I wonder if Nadia sees any similarities between her cult and the Athenaeum's membership, as both are guardians of secret knowledge with their own peculiar rites. Of course, the cult doesn't have public visiting hours.

The Athenaeum library features an exhibit room. Nadia takes me to that room now—the current exhibit is "Portsmouth and World War II." All sorts of interesting naval uniforms and submarine models and schematics are on display. Nadia ignores the exhibit and marches to the far wall, which contains a bunch of memorabilia about four German U-boats surrendering in Portsmouth Harbor in 1945. I already know the story; the Nazi crews were sent to the naval prison across the water, now a crumbling and derelict place with trees growing from its castle-like towers. They say a midnight visitor to the prison would hear spectral moaning in German...

"It's here," Nadia whispers.

"Can you open it *quietly?*" I ask. "And close it quietly, too, from the other side?"

She nods. "Don't worry. But... before I open it, just one last thing."

Uh oh.

Nadia leans in closer. "People over there are capable of magic. Not anything big and flashy or super-powerful, but just, like, dollar magic."

"Excuse me?" I sputter. "Why are you mentioning this only *now*?"

"When would I have had time?" Nadia says. "It's not a big deal. Like... everyone is good at one particular party trick, and it varies by person. It's not strong enough to replace electricity or change the weather or anything. Might be startling at first, that's all."

Startling. Not the word I'd use to describe seeing someone wielding magical powers. Even if it is just "dollar magic," as Nadia says. I'm still mentally reeling from the things I saw in the City of Games—the inexplicable power behind Wagers, the Hand that crushed Chaum with a single finger—and that was weeks ago.

"Good to know," I say, balling my fists. "We need to cross over before we're caught, so..."

"Right." Nadia clears her throat and begins the ritual.

She walks a different pattern than I've seen thus far, tracing a crescent shape on the carpet. The words she's speaking are unintelligible to me, but of course they are; the only Port language I can understand is that of the Hand. Then she opens up a bag stuffed with her offering for this type of Port: feathers. Now I've got a guess as to the Port type.

In the middle of the memorabilia, an old booklet called "Surrender at Sea" trembles. Nadia flings the feathers at the spot, which gobbles them up, sucking them into nothingness. The spot widens—a window to another world opens. Slowly at first, then it grows rapidly in diameter. The hole is surrounded by a whooshing wind, barely visible, but definitely audible. Blowback from the mysterious currents around the Port ruffles my hair.

Yep, it's an air Port. It must be my unhappy destiny to sample all the types of Ports. If the Bloody Swarm holds sway over water-affiliated Ports, and the Hand That Never Closes is master of quintessence Ports, who's in charge of air ones?

I open my mouth to ask the question. Then I forget all about it as I look through the Port, seeing an Athenaeum much like this one— except it's fallen into ruin. Nadia looks at it curiously. "I wonder what—"

"Quiet." The sound of the pen writing below us has stopped. Now footsteps are climbing the stairs. Nadia won't hear them yet, though.

I make a snap decision. "Get on that side of the door," I order Nadia in a low hiss.

Then I hustle over to the other side and flatten myself against the wall. Whoever it is—based on the light footfalls, a woman—I won't *hurt* them. But I can't allow them to interfere with our mission, either.

A grey-haired black woman enters the room, stops dead at the sight of the swirling gate to another universe. She's no assassin from the city council; her outfit and poise suggest a librarian, which she has every right to be, here in the Athenaeum. I press the Glock 26 to her temple.

"Don't move," I say, "and don't turn around."

3

"So... I guess it's true," the woman says, obeying my order and staying still. "Black folks aren't even safe indoors anymore."

I cringe, painfully aware of my own skin. What if my old colleagues at the PD were right, and I *am* a terrorist now? "You'll be safe as long as you do what we say." I try to mask my own voice by pitching it lower, but it doesn't work.

"We? How many of you does it take to subdue a fifty-two-year-old librarian?"

Damn Nadia for not double-checking this place was clear. Nadia's wide mouth is set in a hard line; she's blushing through her freckles. She makes a clubbing motion at me, her hand gripping an invisible pistol by the barrel.

I answer her with a furious head-shake. No, my dear, I can't just "knock someone unconscious" like they do in the movies. The more likely result would be a concussion or worse while my victim remained inconveniently conscious.

The librarian halted at the sight of the Port, but she didn't gasp. Didn't scream. Maybe she's an incredibly self-controlled individual—or maybe not.

"You don't exactly seem surprised to see … this," I say to her. "May I ask why?"

"I'd prefer not to carry on a conversation at gunpoint," the librarian responds, reasonably enough.

"OK, here's what we're gonna do," I say. "You're going to close your eyes, turn right, and walk to the corner of the room. You'll face the corner until the room goes quiet. Then you can turn around, and it'll be like none of this unpleasantness ever happened at all. If you don't follow these instructions, I'll shoot you. Is that clear?"

"Absolutely, Ms. Allard," the librarian says.

Fuck.

The gun drops to my side. The woman slowly turns to look me in the eye. Her face shows no trace of malice I can see.

"How?" I say, defeated.

I'm now alone in the exhibit room with the librarian and the Port. Nadia took the opportunity to duck into the library proper. The librarian glances at the Port. "Your voice was a woman's voice. It was coming from below me, and I'm not a tall person. Now, how many diminutive gun-toting women dealing in the supernatural do we have running around town, Ms. Allard? Please tell me there aren't many more than you."

"So—you've seen this P—this gate before, then?" I ask, gesturing at it. "Do you work for the city council?"

"This is a *private* library; we are independent," she says. "And no, I've never seen this Port before, but I suspected it was there. We could spend a long time comparing notes, indeed I'd love to, but I assume you opened the Port for a reason. I don't want to keep you and your friend from your appointment, whatever it might be."

Then the librarian gazes at the Port, watching the

eldritch winds swirl. "It's... magnificent," she says softly. "Isn't it?"

"I..." My voice trails off. Time *is* of the essence, though I have so many questions. "Would you mind going and facing the corner? My friend's on the shy side."

"Will you shut the 'door' behind you?" she asks.

"Yes."

The librarian nods and goes to the corner. Nadia emerges from the library and strides to the wind-wreathed Port, and both of us step through.

Maybe the cultists enjoy this part: feeling an unearthly tingling in all their limbs and orifices. I do not. For me, it's a sharp reminder of how unnatural these gateways are, joining worlds and universes that would have been better off staying forever apart. When Trig latches onto words like "eigenstates" and wages endless debates about the relative primacy of worlds, he's ignoring the essential wrongness of this breach, this violation. Scientifically supported or not, Ports *should not be*.

My journey in the in-between is only seconds long, but for the first time I feel I'm not alone during the transition. Whatever the master of air Ports is, it's watching me.

I'm standing in the exhibit room of the Portsmouth Athenaeum again, facing the doorway to the library, as if I've been bodily turned around and then spit out back where I came. But this is the Athenaeum$_2$, in Portsmouth$_2$, not the Athenaeum of our world, and here the room is in shambles.

Nadia is looking out at Market Square... not through a window, but through the *wall*, which has crumbled away, leaving this floor of the building exposed. The whole city has experienced a catastrophic event, not just this building. The streets are littered with crushed cars and fallen masonry. The square itself has a gaping sinkhole in the middle. Directly across from us, the iconic white steeple of the North Church has toppled over, lying on the row of buildings to its right. The beautiful stained-glass dome atop the Irish restaurant next to Breaking New Grounds is shattered, looking like a jagged crown.

Amid the wreckage, I do see several survivors. Some are picking their way around the hazards on desperate errands. Some are, predictably, taking advantage of the chaos for their own gain. And now I notice a few figures in naval uniform, though they don't seem overly concerned with the looting.

As the panic flutters in my chest, I remind myself of all those little twos: Market Square$_2$, the North Church$_2$, Portsmouth$_2$. This is not our home.

But as I can see, it is somebody's. Even if these aren't our people, they're still people, and they're suffering.

"What happened here?" I ask.

"I... I have no idea." Nadia stares numbly out at the ruined city. "I swear it wasn't like this before. Did I —did we—?"

"Did you *what*?"

Nadia gives me a brisk head shake, summoning her usual resolve and turning away. "Nothing. You promised that librarian we'd close the Port up right away—I'd better get on it."

"Hold on," I say. "I don't think I want to *stay* here. We're going to have a hard time getting down to Boston-two if all of New England-two looks like this."

"Who's to say it does?" Nadia points out. "The disaster could be limited to Portsmouth. In any case, I at least am sticking around here to find out what the hell happened. This is horrible, Allard."

My stomach gives a sick surge. I can't leave her here in this nightmare alone. "Fine, close it up—as long as you're positive you can get it open again."

Nadia holds up a thick bag of feathers. "Got all I need. Even if the last damn bird in this world is dead, we'll be okay."

As she closes the Port, I give Portsmouth$_2$ another look from this extensive vantage point. This time I notice more details. The sturdier buildings remain standing, like the solid grey Custom House building, which has belonged to the Portsmouth landscape since the early nineteenth century. And there's no sign of Market Square Day festivities —if they do celebrate it here, the devastation must have hit before they set up for the event. Or maybe they celebrate it in June instead of July.

Here the Memorial Bridge has been rebuilt for modern traffic, unlike in our world, where the old version of the bridge was torn down and we're still waiting for the new. Giant silver spheres grace the two bridge towers flanking the lift span in the middle; they have pupils carved into them, like they're eyes. However, the fancy new construction here has met its match—the bridge is twisted and unsafe, much like the downtown roads themselves.

Eyes. What an odd design feature for a bridge. But now I'm realizing other odd touches: the downed North Church tower is topped not by a cross, but by a crescent shape, like a moon. And the coffeeshop where Breaking New Grounds should be is called Eye Widener's. A different business altogether occupies the corner of the Custom House building, where the Portsmouth Book and Bar should be. In place of the square Book and Bar sign, there's... well, a crescent-shaped sign with a picture of something I can't discern.

"Let's go."

Nadia's generous mouth is set in determination, her dark brows knitted. Her steadiness inspires the same in me, and I say, "All right. "First thing—we find out what the fuck happened, and quickly, in case it's still happening."

We enter the wrecked library of the Athenaeum, the floor littered with books. If I were truly interested in alternate history, this would be the place to scoop up some reading material—what's up with the crescent in place of a cross? At what point or points did our timelines diverge, and how did the presence of "dollar magic" affect the flow of history?

Fascinating stuff for a woman who isn't on a mission. I head for the stairs, which are descendable even if no longer OSHA-certified. Nadia's a couple steps ahead of me. We enter the square and get a ground-level look at the devastation.

It wasn't a nuke. At least, I don't think it was. The city would be leveled, not half-leveled. Same if it had been the Seabrook nuclear plant blowing. No, this was caused by a level of tectonic activity unprecedented for southern New Hampshire since the days of Pangaea. The damage coming from *below,* not above.

Why did I let myself walk right into this nightmareland? Nadia's got my head turned around. And she wasn't *that* good of a kisser. Damn, I truly have been getting soft.

Nadia has managed to trap a survivor in conversation, a middle-aged woman wearing a plaid jacket despite the heat. The woman looks at us with renewed panic. "Where did you two come from?"

"Away," Nadia says.

"Bullcrap," says the woman. "Maine was hit too. But you ladies look like you stepped off a modeling shoot for Feathered Lady. *Where* are you from?"

"Another world," I say impatiently.

"Ah. Wishful thinking. Wish I could fantasize my way out of this hellscape, too. So what are you, know-it-alls? Creeps? Heartburners? Whatever your ability, we could use your help. A powerful know-it-all would be a real blessing from Fath—we need to know if they're going to hit again, and if so, when."

"Ability?" I say, feeling lost. "Know-it-alls? What exactly happened here?"

"The *spiders* happened," the woman moans. "The spiders, Fath-dammit! What do you *think*?!"

Spiders. Never my favorite animal. Not even my favorite arachnid. But... "This all was caused by *spiders*?"

Her eyes narrow. "Thephal's owl, you really are from another world."

Nadia looks paler than usual. "What kind of spiders are you talking about?"

"Listen, I've got to help with relief efforts," the woman says. "I don't have time to stand around arguing with idiots!"

With that, she scurries off.

"Nadia," I say, "you were wondering something when we first stepped through—then you cut yourself off. Do you think *you* could be responsible for whatever happened here?"

She considers the question without deflecting. "I was the one who first discovered this Port. I bear responsibility for anything that happens to people here as a result of the Port." She pauses. "Have you ever heard of the anxiety of influence, Divya? It's real when it comes to Ports. We can change worlds just by visiting them... by *observing* them."

"Anxiety's a state of mind," I say. "The observer effect is documented science, though, isn't it? So you guys are awfully irresponsible to keep opening Ports!"

A haunted look flits across her face. Then she gets mulish. "If you knew—goddammit, if explorers and scientists were too afraid to affect anything, then where would we be today?"

"You and I? Not standing in an alternate nightmare version of our poor city."

"We can assign all the proper blame later. Right now, let's figure out how far this catastrophe reaches."

The two of us approach a man picking through a scavenged storefront on Congress Street. It's a fancy restaurant back in our world, but here it's a kitchen supply shop. The cracked wooden marquee features an illustration of a colonial white dude I can't identify. As we get closer, I can hear the scavenger muttering, "Has to be *something* good in here..."

"Hey," I say to him, as gently as I can manage. "Can we talk?"

He freezes without turning around.

There's no telling how people will react in this hellscape. They're understandably traumatized by the destruction of Portsmouth$_2$. I ease Jeong's Glock 26 out of its holster, and Nadia notices.

"This isn't the most diplomatic approach," she frets.

I walk slowly toward the man, whose right arm darts toward something unseen. "I've got a gun," I say. "If you're reaching for a weapon, you'd be well advised to drop it."

The crouching man gives us a pained grimace. I realize he's one of the city councilors—Jack Wegman. The one whose daughter Val went missing last year. He's holding a pocketknife. Nadia steps back; apparently she's recognized him too. No city councilor can be trusted, after they've made so many Portwalkers disappear...

No, I remind myself, *this is not the Wegman I think I know. This is Wegman$_2$.*

Abruptly my panic recedes—and I'm not sure why. I feel like I've been slipped one of my happy pills. I glance at Nadia, and she has a similarly perplexed look. Then her dark brows rise.

"I feel weird too," she says. "He could be a heartburner. Heartburners can irritate what we're feeling—or dampen our feelings—or even introduce new emotions into people. But this guy's only got a dollar-magic version."

"I don't want any trouble," Wegman$_2$ says in a rusty voice. He lets the pocketknife he's holding fall to the pitted sidewalk.

"We're not here to give you trouble," I say, using a much lighter tone than I intended. My upper lip twists as I attempt to control my own emotions; I don't appreciate being SSRI'ed. "If you're messing with our heads at all right now, *stop* it. Please."

He gives us a small nod. The invisible damper on my fear and anger is released; the surge of negative emotions returning makes me unsteady.

I lower the Glock but keep it handy. "Can you tell us who's in charge here? Is it the military? I saw a few soldiers earlier."

"Nah, not the military. All they care about is their damn shipyard and airbase. We're on our own now... there's a young woman. Dark-skinned. Don't know her name. You want to go... over to the Eostrix. Place with the owl sign." He points at the Custom House building.

Then Wegman$_2$ gives us another look. "Who—who are you? You both look so *clean.* Where were you hiding out?"

"Elsewhere," I say. "Thank you kindly for the information, Councilor Wegman."

"Councilor?" the man says, laughing. "The fuck you hear that from?"

We leave him to resume his rummaging. I turn to Nadia. "I could use some elaboration on this 'dollar magic' thing. Before someone else pulls a mystical mind-grope on me."

She nods reluctantly, brushes her hair out of her face. "Like I said before, these aren't sophisticated spells by any means. They're... little tricks most people here learn to use when they're kids, by harnessing the tide inside them."

The tide. I look at her sharply. "Scott Shaughnessy used that term. For his little rod that he used to control people—he called it the tidal rod. He said he was pulling at a person's tide."

"Keep in mind," Nadia says, "that I may strangle myself thanks to the geas. You sure you can't put it all together on your own, Detective?"

Shaughnessy's little set of nightmare tools—the Mesmerist's Toolset—is currently in a safe deposit box at the bank underneath my apartment, and that's where I intend for it to stay. Still, I wish I knew how the tidal rod *works*. If the people here in Earth$_2$ use their "tide" to perform magic, however minor, then...

"So could we—people from *our* world—perform magic too if we knew how to harness our own tide?" I ask.

She gives me a crooked smile. "Now you're on to something. Although maybe people in this world are born with stronger tides."

"And what *is* a tide? What is it made of? Is it our souls?"

Nadia shrugs. "You got me there. Even with all my travels, I'm a kid playing under the clothing racks in this great department store we call the multiverse."

Something new occurs to me. "Patricia Gagnon told me the story behind the Mesmerist's Toolset. But she never told me what, uh, element the Port leading to that world was. Given the use of the word 'tide,' I'm gonna say it was water."

"Domain of the Bloody Swarm," she says. "Of the five Port masters, the Bloody Swarm is the trickster. The manipulator."

"Cool guy."

"I mean... not a guy, or a girl. More of a supreme being beyond space and time."

I wouldn't think of the Hand That Never Closes as male or female, either, just a terrifying omnipotent creature that's taken up residence in a corner of my mind. "Please pass on my apologies," I say.

"Maybe you can convey them yourself, someday," she says.

We make our way to Eostrix. The crescent-shaped sign outside shows an owl, as Wegman$_2$ mentioned. Perhaps *Thephal's owl,* as the woman in plaid said, or maybe they're just big on owls around here. Bricks and other wrecked stuff litter the wide, flat stone steps beneath the front door, but someone has kept the path to the entrance clear.

Before we enter, Nadia halts and grabs my arm.

"Are you sure you—" she mutters, then stops, knuckles her chin. "What if you run into yourself in there? The Divya of this world could be in charge here."

"Wegman said a *young* woman. Now look at this craggy face."

"Seriously," Nadia presses. "You've had enough trouble with doppelgängers for one lifetime. Do you want me to check out the situation first?"

I snort. "Thanks, but are *you* prepared for the possibility of Nadia$_2$?"

Fear flashes in her eyes. But what could she fear from herself? "Don't worry," I say, amused at turning the reassurance around. "Not all twins are evil. Benazir wasn't the greatest example—but I believe there may be some measure of redemption even for her. Why else go through all this trouble to rescue her?"

Nadia bites her lip. Goddamn, I wouldn't mind taking a nibble on that lip either.

Down, girl. Thephal's owl, this is no time to be horny.

"You're right, I'm no chickenshit, and neither are you," she says, taking a deep breath and exhaling loudly. "I'll assume the best of you from this point on, and you do the same for me. Deal?"

"Deal," I say. I clasp her hand and hold it for too long. She notices, quickly kisses my fingers, and then frees her own hand. She leads the way into the Eostrix.

Chaos reigns in the interior of the store. It's neither a bookstore nor a bar: though it does feature some books, the Eostrix primarily focuses on New Age-type crystals and other knick-knacks. The signs on the walls advertise "guaranteed" methods for enhancing one's natural gifts. Blood scent suffuses the air, and people are screaming in pain. All of the shelves and displays have been pushed aside to make room for cots; panicked amateur nurses race to treat the wounded. A haphazard arrangement of medical supplies lines the register counter.

I know many of these people from my world by sight, whether from my former life as a cop or passing them on the downtown streets. There's the guy who does a brisk business selling watercolors to tourists in front of the bank in the summertime—here he's grey-faced and clutching his chest. The woman who always walks around town wearing a trenchcoat and sunglasses—you called her The Spy, though she's probably just cracked in the head—here her trademark coat is spattered with blood, her head bandaged, eyes squinting without her shades. The local lookalike for a certain Hollywood leading man, the kindly sandwich maker from the place on State Street, the artist with her tiny downtown gallery: they're all here, and they're all fighting for their lives.

It *hurts* to see so many familiar faces in agony; my mind refuses to see them as mere alternates of the people I know. And all because of...

the spiders

I grit my teeth. Spiders my ass.

That's when I catch sight of Solomon Shrive. One of his legs is gone.

No, no, no, no, no. My own legs turn to jelly as I lurch toward the young man lying on a cot. A black woman in her fifties attends to him. Sol_2's left leg has been amputated—maybe it got caught under something heavy. One of his arms looks twisted, too. He's already breathing hard, but as soon as he sees me his panic turns to terror.

"*Divya!*" he screams.

All activity in the makeshift hospital halts. Everyone looks at Sol_2 and me. Sol_2 struggles to sit up, but the woman pushes him back down, muttering, "Stay, stay, for your own good, kid, stay!"

I realize she's the librarian from our world, but it hardly seems to matter. Sol's good arm flies up and thrust a raw, skinned finger in my direction.

"*I saw you die,*" he moans. The moan turns into a wail. "*I saw you die!!*"

Dozens of eyes have paralyzed me to the spot. Even Nadia is out of suggestions. I say shakily, "I guess it didn't take."

"Relax, kid," the $librarian_2$ at his side murmurs. "You've been through hell. You must not have seen what you thought you did."

"I *know* what I *saw!*" Sol$_2$ screams. "I *know* what I *saw!*" He thrashes out of the woman's grasp and forces himself to sit upright, then screams once again, this time from pain.

"Ryder, help!" the woman shouts. "I need a sedative over here, now!"

Another woman bursts out of the back room, her hands full of supplies. Young, also a woman of color. I watch her cross the room and give the librarian$_2$ a quick slap of reassurance on the shoulder before plunging a syringe into Sol$_2$'s arm. He collapses back against her and she lays him down gently. Then she looks up at me with furious eyes.

Hannah.

"Who are you?" she demands. "Why in Fath the Giver's name are you upsetting this patient?"

My world is spinning. Despite all my assurances to Nadia, I'm *not* ready for this world. Because you, Hannah Ryder, are standing right in front of me, alive and well. And you have no idea who I am.

4

No. You're Hannah Ryder$_2$—not *my* Hannah. I have to keep that crucial fact front and center in my mind or I'll lose it.

Still, the fact that you're an *exact copy* is so hard to ignore. Your cloud of stiff black hair, your rich dark-brown skin (I loved the way our colors looked side by side, flesh on flesh), your bright and searching eyes, your curves, your nose-ring... your stubborn stance, your *voice*...

"I'm... D-Divya," I stutter. I decide to usurp the dead Divya Allard$_2$'s place, however repellent an action it might be. "I survived the incident. Sol's just delirious."

Hannah$_2$ looks at me blankly. "Good for you. You here to help or to rubberneck? If the latter, get the fuck out of here."

Nadia takes me by the arm in a smooth motion. I'm too dazed to resist. "We're here to help," she says.

"*No*, we're not," I say. "We need to ask a few questions."

"Are you sure the shipyard boys didn't send you?" Hannah$_2$ asks. "Because you can tell them again, this is our place. They don't get to take it over. And we don't respond kindly to threats."

You wouldn't abandon people in a disaster, either. You wouldn't knuckle under to some brass-balled fuck no matter how many medals were pinned to his chest.

"We're free agents," I say. "Trust me."

Hannah$_2$'s hostility has vanished. Now she's all business. "Get Mr. Praeger a dose of corticosteroids and then bring over some more jugs of water from the back hall. Do that and *maybe* I'll find someone to answer questions for you."

"Will do," Nadia says. Then she hisses in my ear, "Divya, so you're clear that that's not her, right?"

"I know," I say. "I know, I know, I know." If I keep saying it, I'll believe it. Not you. Not you. But you can't *not* be you... I keep mentally tripping over the double negatives and double presences of you, dead and alive—like me, alive and dead. You and I, we're Schrödinger's cats, aren't we?

I shake off the turmoil in my head and say, "Nadia, she didn't recognize me. Does that mean that here—"

"Yeah, you know exactly what it means," Nadia murmurs. "Here, she may have never even *met* you. Don't assume your relationship, or anyone's relationship, transcends the branching paths of the multiverse. Anything can happen."

Hannah$_2$ is someone I've never taken into my arms, never loved, never fucked, never promised my future to. A stranger.

"Hannah-two, Hannah-two, Hannah-two," I mutter. "If I say it enough times, maybe it'll finally penetrate."

As I'm trying to figure out who "Mr. Praeger" is, I see Hannah$_2$ isn't the only one leading the relief efforts. While Hannah$_2$ is the firecracker keeping the front lines going, a familiar imposing, iron-jawed figure is sorting out medical supplies at the counter. She scribbles notes in a notebook and then marks a sheet taped to the wall, which looks like a makeshift schedule for the "nurses."

"Hey! Get back outside, Pete," Milly Fragonard says, reaching over the counter and collaring a young man I don't recognize—a kid—in one easy motion. "You're on thief-busting duty until nightfall. You still have your boomstick?"

"Yes, ma'am," says the young man.

"So—where *is* it?"

"Sorry, I'm on it," he babbles, and he hurries past us. Pete ducks down behind a desk and comes up with a shotgun. I flinch, but no one else here reacts; they're either not looking or they've seen worse. The kid hustles outside to take up sentry duty. Then I turn back to Milly—

No! Milly$_2$, dammit. This Milly still has her eyes. Completely different woman than the one I served with on the force. For all I know, this one's never worn a uniform, though her carriage suggests otherwise. Nevertheless, the familiarity of Milly$_2$'s face makes me want to run to her. She's a solid rock in this foaming sea of uncertainty. I'm sure she can answer our questions without preconditions, unlike Hannah$_2$. But...

"Maybe we should just *go*," I say. "We're wasting time."

"If we hit the road without knowing what we're getting into," Nadia says, "we're as good as dead. *Giant spiders*, remember?"

Without waiting for me to agree, she calls out, "Milly!"

Milly$_2$ looks at us suspiciously. "Sorry—do I know you?"

Interesting. Either she or I—Allard$_2$—never became a police officer. "We're new in town," I say, "and we wanted to know... how widespread is this thing with the spiders? Is it happening in Boston too?"

Milly$_2$ stiffens. "This was the epicenter, as far as I know, but it's spread *everywhere*... which you should know, for

God's sake! Which direction did you come from that *wasn't* affected?"

"These people bothering you, Milly?" Hannah$_2$ places herself between Milly$_2$ and us. "Knew there was something off about 'em. I think they're spies for the goddamn Navy. I'll haul their asses out right now."

I know I won't be able to fight back, won't be able to resist if she does. As soon as she lays her hands on me, I'll dissolve. I'll be a puddle on the floor of the Eostrix.

But Milly$_2$ holds up her hand. "Wait. I could believe that this one—" she gestures at me— "is from the military, but the blonde? No. She's jacked, but she's no spy. She wouldn't be dumb enough to call me by my name without knowing me."

"Thank you," says Nadia with a sardonic smile.

Milly$_2$ reaches down and draws a gun on us: her service weapon from the PD, a Sig 226. Yep, she's definitely a cop here. Hannah$_2$ steps away from us. Nadia and I freeze in place.

"Doesn't mean they're not dangerous," she says. "Spies I understand... *this,* I don't. Two strangers in clean clothes who have no idea what's going on. You've got thirty seconds to explain your deal. Go."

"You want the truth?" I say.

"Try me."

"We come from an alternate Portsmouth, in another world, and we need to get down to Boston in your world."

Milly$_2$'s lip quivers. Her grip tightens on her pistol. "That's what you're going with?"

"Giant spiders, Milly," I say. "Bet *that* didn't seem possible to you before they arrived."

"Neither of them's a mindfucker," she says to Hannah$_2$. "I'd be able to tell. They aren't trying anything."

"What are they?" Hannah₂ says.

Milly₂ peers at us, half-lidded. "Short one's a creep. Wait... the blonde *is* a mindfucker, but it's like she's never even used her tide before. That's why I didn't spot it at first."

"Excuse me?" I say. "Did you call me a *creep*?"

"I think you're missing the point," Nadia hisses at me.

Now Milly₂ gives Hannah₂ a sidelong glance with clear meaning: *I told you so*. But told her what? Hannah₂'s eyes widen and she takes a cautious step toward us.

"An alternate Portsmouth," she says slowly. "Where none of this happened?"

Careful. I see a yearning in her eyes I recognize. That's the patented Hannah Ryder "Get out of Dodge, I don't care where" look—the look that crystallizes your mindset before meeting me, the solution to every major problem you encountered. You used to be a nomad, and I know now that you never outgrew it. I thought you had embraced staying in one place, with me, but instead you'd turned your gaze toward other universes instead of other cities and states.

"Yes," I say, and that's all I say.

Then Nadia adds, "We can sh—"

I grab her wrist so hard she cries out in pain.

Nadia's face is so full of unexpected rage that I let go and backpedal. She looks like a stranger, as unfamiliar to me as my own features on Benazir's face when they were twisted by hate. Then her dark eyebrows rise, her eyes soften, and Milly₂ says, "Ahem."

"Maybe I forgot to mention it, but *don't move*," Milly₂ barks at us. Her P226 remains trained on us. "If you're not lying, how did you get here?"

The door in the back opens. I consider using the second of distraction to attempt to wrestle the gun away from her. But A), Milly₂ shares my training and I don't like my odds of survival, and B) the thirtysomething guy sauntering into the field hospital has the power to distract *me*. It's Zeke Briard—urgh, Zeke Briard$_2$—the alternate version of a sort-of friend back home, albeit one I haven't seen much since my fall from grace.

Zeke, with his sandy blond hair and his easy white smile, has the power of charm both in my world and this one. It's a harder feat for the Zeke$_2$ version to pull off amid an arachnid apocalypse, but he's doing it, all right; heads turn and smiles appear across the room, even from the direly wounded. Hannah$_2$'s smile is the widest of all. Indeed, as Nadia and I both watch, Zeke$_2$ walks to Hannah$_2$, takes her in his arms, and kisses her full on her unresisting lips.

"You son of a bitch," I hiss before I realize what I'm saying.

The couple separates. Zeke$_2$, half-grinning, says, "Haven't heard that one in a while. Don't tell me you're *jealous,* Divya, in the middle of this nightmare?"

"Babe," Hannah$_2$ says, gripping his shoulder, "whoever you think this is, it's probably not her."

"I already know you're a serial cheater," I say to him, extrapolating from the Zeke I know, "but I never expected you to draw someone like Hannah into it. And Hannah, you should be better than this."

Now Milly$_2$ breaks in: "But who's *Annah?*"

My jaw drops. Hannah$_2$ fails to jump in and claim the name, or its close cousin, and I realize yet another assumption I've been making, one that Trig maybe could have warned me against. The woman whose name I thought I knew says, "I'm Arreth."

"Fuck," Nadia whispers. "Divya, I *told* you not to think everything would be the same…"

Arreth. I could see Hannah being a Julia or a Naomi

instead, but what kind of a name is Arreth? "So are you not Zeke either, then?" I ask.

"Zeke?" he says with a laugh. "What? No, I'm Gaff. What's wrong with you, Divya?"

Gaff?!

"Uh," I say. "'Arreth' is right ... I'm not the Divya you think you know. It sounds like the Divya Allard of this world died."

Gaff pales. "What do you mean, died? *You're right here.*"

My head is spinning. I'm having increasing trouble keeping our worlds apart. If Hannah$_2$—*Arreth*—had to be in a relationship, I would have preferred it be with a stranger. Zeke Briard is supposed to be married to Emma Briard. But this guy's name is Gaff, so who the hell knows? And what was *Gaff*'s relationship to Divya$_2$? Don't tell me I was programmed for men here...

Evidently the same thought occupies Arreth's mind. Her lips pursing, she asks him, "How exactly did you know, um, Divya?"

Gaff looks away from her. Good gods. This world is going to be a *lot* harder than I thought.

"Excuse me," Milly$_2$ says. "You haven't told me how you got here."

Nor should we. I can only imagine the mad rush for a world *not* devastated by mutant spiders that would commence. If a hundred walking wounded came home with Nadia and me, out of nowhere... how would we ever explain it? Where would they go? I grit my teeth and say, "A gateway. It's not important."

"Not important?" Arreth asks. "I'd rather be where you're from than stick around here any longer. And all these people deserve better medical care than the barebones treatment we're giving them."

"You're a know-it-all," Milly$_2$ tells her. "You're a geek. Can't you see into their past?"

Arreth takes these seeming insults in stride, looking at us closely. "I'll try."

As Arreth concentrates on us, Milly$_2$ says, "You sure you need to go down to Boston? You're going to get yourselves killed long before you get there."

I sigh. If the spiders have devastated all of New England$_2$, as she claims, then yes, that does put a significant crimp in our mission.

"Let's say we do need to," I say. "What would it take for us to survive?"

Milly$_2$ looks at us doubtfully. "You'd need to know the spiders' movements. Know when they're going to strike a place, so you could get out of the way. I'm... aware of someone who can sometimes hear the spiders' voices in her head. She could provide you with exactly the information you need, but she's unavailable. Find someone else with similar magic, and you might get down to the City of Notions in one piece."

"How? Where could we find—"

But clear-eyed Arreth cuts me off with a loud "Fath's balls!" She sucks in her breath. "They *are* telling the truth. I saw... the gateway she spoke of. We need to find it."

I can't believe she really *did* see into our past...

Then I hear a shout from outside the Eostrix. A gun discharges—a shotgun—followed by a phalanx of armed men in naval service dress whites entering the store. I'm afraid for what happened to poor young Pete out there, but more pressingly, I'm afraid for myself and for Nadia.

I grab her arm and pull her around the corner to flatten both of us against the wall, out of the path of the sailors, who pay us little mind. They're screaming "Drop it! Drop it!"

and holding up their P228s and 12-gauge Mossberg shotguns.

Arreth and Gaff raise their hands in surrender, and several of the patients and amateur nurses cry out in fear. But Milly$_2$ remains perfectly calm, keeping her P226 raised in defiance of the sailors' commands. "Drop yours first," she says. "The heck you people think you are?"

The man leading the pack is soft-featured with a cold, professional gaze. His black-and-gold-brimmed hat is fancier than those of the other sailors and his chest is bristling with ribbons. He raises a hand to keep his men from firing. "I'm Command Master Chief Brooks, United States Navy. We are commandeering this building in the name of the United States government. Put your weapon down, Officer Fragonard."

Milly$_2$ raises an eyebrow. "Why does everyone know my name today?"

"Word gets around about the woman who can hear those monsters' thoughts," Command Master Chief (CMDCM) Brooks says. "Maybe even talk back to them. You could be useful to your country in this time of crisis. I.e., it'd be a shame to put a hole in you, ma'am, so would you please...?"

Hm. Milly$_2$ failed to mention *she* was the one who can hear the spiders thinking. Nadia looks like she wants to jump into the conversation, but I hold her back. I've got Ethan's piece in my waistband, but that's only good against one opponent, maybe two if I'm not rusty. Not six.

"This is a hospital," Milly$_2$ says. "I get the feeling that's not your priority, though."

"It could be one of our priorities if you let us," Brooks says. "You could use better resources, could you not?"

"You don't give a, a *crap* about these people. You didn't

lift a finger to help us in the aftermath. We had to help ourselves. And now, what, you—"

"There's no reason for you to distrust us," the CMDCM says gently. "You need not have any suspicions."

She squints at him and says, "A heartburner, huh. That's not gonna work on me. Maybe the rumor mill left out the part about me being one of the best blockers in Portsmouth."

Without a word, another of the sailors steps forward. I watch him, confused about his silent look of concentration, and then Sol_2 shrieks: "*Spider!!*"

A massive shape blots out the grey light from the windows of the Eostrix. I glimpse a hairy brown limb, a set of wicked mandibles or pincers, and then everyone is screaming. Pandemonium ensues as all the patients that can move try to do so, away from the windows, and the nurses grab those who can't and drag them off their cots.

Despite my own terror, I note the sailors don't seem scared of the spider outside—and neither does $Milly_2$. She bellows at her patients and nurses, "It's an illusion! Stop this right now! This guy's a mindfucker! He—"

Crack! $Milly_2$'s hand flies to her neck. Blood erupts from between her fingers; she sways on her feet. Her mouth opens and more blood pours out. She drops the Sig 226 and falls behind the counter.

The spider beyond the windows winks out of existence. The sailor $Milly_2$ called a "mindfucker" rubs his temples and shakes his head. Command Master Chief Brooks whirls to another sailor, the one who fired, a frightened-looking petty officer. "What have you done?" he shrieks in the petty officer's face. "Do you know what you've done?"

No. Clearly he doesn't. I hear another gunshot ring out, different-sounding than the first—maybe someone scooped up Milly$_2$'s pistol to return fire on the sailors. In any case, Nadia and I don't need to see how this ends.

I shove her toward the door and we both take off running. My shoulders are hunched in the expectation of a bullet hitting me from behind. None does, though the screams and hoarse yells must mean more victims are dropping. We make it out into the street. We don't look behind us until we've taken refuge behind a partially collapsed wall near the remains of the Friendly Toast—here known as the Grinning Pancake.

∽

NADIA IS TREMBLING, but her voice is steady when she speaks: "They killed her. Fascist bastards killed her."

"What's a blocker?" I ask. It's the only question to rise from the muddled stew of my mind. My cheek is wet: someone else's blood.

My companion knuckles the corner of her eye. "They —*block*. You know, magic."

"Milly didn't block that, what did she say, that mindfucker? She didn't block him from creating that illusion of a big-ass spider."

"She blocked herself from getting fooled by it. And she blocked the heartburner when he tried to manipulate her emotions, get her to trust him."

Heartburner. Mindfucker. And… "Milly called Hannah, or rather Arreth, a know-it-all. We heard that expression elsewhere too. Is that another type of… magical person here? What do *they* do?"

All of this, uh, technical talk is doing a great deal to calm us both down. Nadia nods at me, glad for the question. "You remember, she asked Arreth to look into our past—she meant a few minutes into it. The know-it-alls can see a little into the past, or the future. Depends on the person. And when she called you a 'creep,' that wasn't an insult, or not exactly."

"Yeah, I can see that now," I say. "But *I* don't have any magic."

"Don't you?" Nadia asks softly. "You met with a god. It did you a favor in your time of need. You sure some of that divine stuff didn't rub off on you?"

Can't be. But I recall what Nadia said earlier, about how maybe even people from our world could harness their own "tide" if properly instructed. "Well, what's a creep do?"

"Infuse life. Or take it away. But again, only on a dollar-magic kinda level. Maybe if you get good at it, you could heal someone's papercut?"

I sigh. "Well. Where does this leave us? Milly-two was right—we're almost definitely going to get killed before we reach Boston-two… if not by a dipshit with a gun or a stupid magic trick, then by these monster spiders. If they look anything like that guy's *illusion* of one…"

Nadia tugs at her blonde locks. "Yeah, too bad the one person who can communicate with the spiders just got shot to death." Her mouth twists at her own bitter sarcasm. "Sorry, Divya. That must have been awful to witness."

A dumb, irresponsible idea hurtles out of my head. It escapes my lips before I can stop it. "Milly-two may not be the only person who can hear the beasties coming."

She looks at me. "Huh?"

"We still have Milly-one."

Comprehension dawns, and she shakes her head sharply. "Allard. No!"

"What if we could bring *our* Milly here and awaken her… tide? She could be our spider-whisperer."

"Our Milly is blind," Nadia protests. "Do you want to endanger another person from our world?"

"We can give her the choice," I say. "We're not going to force her into anything."

Nadia takes a deep breath. "I don't—dammit, this doesn't feel right." She's quiet, looking across the street at a smashed building; I realize it's Jacobi Investment Advisors, my former employer. Although here it's Yathuri, not Jacobi.

Finally, Nadia says, "She's your friend. I guess it's your prerogative. But would she put her life on the line for the sake of Benazir, of all people?"

A fair point. Benazir Allard is the woman who murdered several of Milly's fellow officers. Milly witnessed the blood and madness. "We have to try."

"All right," Nadia mutters. "If she has any sense at all, she'll say no. Hell, if I had any sense at all, I'd take the opportunity to stay home when we go back for her."

I touch her arm. "You can. You *should*. You'd have to be insane to go down to Boston-two with me, after what we've seen here."

Her fingers cover my own. She fixes her startling green eyes on me. "You don't have the market on insanity cornered, Divya."

I'm about to kiss her before I remember what a, well, *insanely* inappropriate situation we're in right now. I withdraw my hand and say, "You may change your mind when we're on the other side. How's the coast looking?"

Nadia is closer to the edge of the wall. She peeks out. "Don't see any Navy guys. We'll want to watch the corner with Pleasant Street when we get closer to Market Square, but... I think we're clear."

I cock an ear to listen. It's hard to distinguish footsteps

from all of the sliding and crumbling of insecure structures. I'll have to trust in her assessment.

We move.

As we slink back down ruined Congress Street, I glimpse a couple sailors on the other side of the square, but they're not on lookout. Instead, they look to be hustling cartons of supplies in the direction of the Eostrix. Nadia and I are able to enter the Athenaeum through its shattered reading room without being noticed or disturbed. I recall that the reading room in our world featured a number of rare historical artifacts, including a decree signed by King George III on the wall. Would the documents be the same here?

Arreth. Gaff. Yathuri. My brain itches to unwind the history of this place, to follow the clues and trace the divergences...

But no, everything in the room is buried under rubble or shattered beyond recognition, and that includes all the hanging items. And Nadia is a few steps ahead of me, looking back with clear impatience. What the hell am I doing? This world is no mystery to solve, just an obstacle to overcome.

I hurry to catch up with her. We ascend to the exhibit room off the library on the upper floor. Nadia digs out her bag of feathers, begins the ritual.

Then I hear them: clear despite the sounds of unsettling and settling amid them. Sneaky footsteps.

"We were followed," I hiss. "And they're coming. Hurry!"

Nadia shoots me a venomous look and continues at the same pace, walking and chanting, casting the feathers. The Port slowly opens. Okay, some shit can't be rushed.

Someone ascends the damaged stairs. The Port is open now, and Nadia charges through it first. I start toward it, but it's too late—our pursuer bursts into the room.

It's Arreth. Half her magnificent curls are matted with blood, but she's alive and apparently unhurt. She holds up a trembling finger at the Port.

"It *is* true!"

This—this is an unfortunate complication.

No, this is a disaster, you snarl in my mind. As if you've been awakened by the sight of your alternate.

I hold my hands up. "Listen, Han—Arreth. We'll be back—you hang tight here, okay?"

You were always *fast*. Before I can grab her, she's hurtled through the Port.

Cursing, I follow her.

—it's watching me—

A few wrenching seconds later, I arrive in the exhibit room of the non-ruined Athenaeum, back in our world. A tableau of three figures faces each other warily: Nadia Chopin, Arreth of Portsmouth$_2$, and the Athenaeum librarian. I sense coiled violence in the first two and mere bewilderment from the third.

"You brought a guest," says the librarian.

"This place is whole," says Arreth. "You have no spiders here."

"Divya!" says Nadia.

I shrug. "Sorry—couldn't catch her."

Arreth breaks the standoff by running to the window. She exclaims under her breath as she peers out at the vibrant Market Square Day celebration.

I hesitate before going to Arreth; I look at the librarian. "You made a phone call, didn't you? Councilors' thugs are waiting for us downstairs, aren't they?"

The librarian, whose alternate worked desperately to save the lives of the wounded back in Portsmouth$_2$, gives me a grimace. "Don't know what you're talking about. This is a private library—I don't work for the city council. Nor was I aware that they have... thugs, as you put it."

I take in the sight of a chair nearby. A plastic container of carrot sticks is sitting on it. "Then why were you hanging around waiting for us to come back?"

"So suspicious, Ms. Allard," says the woman. "I simply want to know more about what you found. Over there. My area of research interest happens to intersect..." She looks over at the Port and shivers at what she sees. "Though I don't think I'll want to do any gathering of primary sources myself."

The librarian approaches me and offers her hand. "I didn't get to introduce myself before. I'm Deah Sloane, Assistant Keeper of the Athenaeum."

I glance impatiently at Arreth, who's goggling at the sights through the window. "I don't have time to indulge you right now," I say to Deah. "We've got—problems layered on problems. Starting with that one right there."

Arreth turns back to us. "This here problem isn't going to go away, ladies. I don't know what this place is, or how we managed to get from—there to here." She casts an uneasy look at the Port. "But your world looks *safe*, and I swore to help a whole lot of injured and desperate people however I could. I'm going to bring them all through."

5

Uh oh.

"No way," Nadia says. "I'm sorry, but if a bunch of homeless and injured people show up in this city—some of them looking *exactly like* existing residents—it'll totally blow our cover."

"Our," of course, meaning Nadia's secret organization, most of whom live in fear of the city council's pocketed cops and hired brutes. I don't blame her for shooting down Arreth's plan, but Arreth is seriously messing with my own judgment. I'm afraid if I open my mouth, I'm gonna make promises to your lookalike that I can't keep. I always had a hard time saying no to you.

Nadia picks up on my hesitation. "Divya? Back me up here!"

"She's right," I say, looking at a picture of Nazi Lieutenant Ulrich Kessler.

"Hello? Who's right?" Arreth demands.

Deah Sloane munches on her carrot sticks and watches us.

I force myself to look Arreth in the eye. "We're in the

middle of something right now. We have to save my... sister, so you're gonna have to wait."

Arreth balls her hands into fists. "*Wait?* My people are under attack! My own boyfriend got shot to death right in front of me, so don't you tell me to fucking *wait!*"

"I've got a gun too," I tell her, and she stops in her tracks. The hurt betrayal on her face is almost enough to make me blabber: *But don't worry, honey, I'd never use it on you!*

"We'll do our best to help you," Nadia says, "in your own world. But you have to trust us. We're bringing in someone who can communicate with the spiders."

I can't believe that Nadia has made that promise—*I'm* supposed to be the sucker. Arreth asks, "Like Milly?"

"Very much like Milly," Nadia answers with bitter amusement.

"Dammit, Nadia," I snap, "we're getting further and further away from our goal here. We can't—"

"Allard, please," she says. She gives me a meaningful look. As far as what the meaning is, I can't be sure... *This is only our option for dealing with this troublemaker*? *We owe it to her*? Or *I'm lying through my teeth to her and you should be able to tell*?

"You're legit gonna help me," Arreth says.

"Yes," Nadia says.

"But our first priority is getting out of here," I break in. "There's some unfriendly folks in the crowd down there who we should definitely avoid..."

"You'll find our back exit convenient, then," Deah says. "Let me show you."

Arreth raises an eyebrow at Nadia and me and says, "You guys make friends wherever you go, huh?"

"Something like that," I say. The three of us follow the librarian to a flight of back stairs leading down through the

Athenaeum; I notice there's also a tiny elevator, though it wouldn't hold more than two of us at a time.

"It is July here, isn't it?" Arreth asks. "You're holding Summerwind Fest late. Should be the second Saturday in June."

"Uh, what?" Then I realize she's talking about Market Square Day. "That's not what we call it here."

Arreth scoffs. "No? Don't you even *acknowledge* Fath in your version? I didn't see a single eye float or owl banner out there."

Before I can think how to answer that, Deah says, "This way," and opens the door to the courtyard at the rear of the building. The courtyard's open at the back side, but chain-link gates topped with barbed wire block the exit.

"You'll be able to leave out that way," she says, "which will take you to Ladd Street. Duck through the parking garage and come out on Hanover Street and you should avoid detection altogether. By whoever's looking for you... I'm not sure I want to know."

She crosses the courtyard and fishes a key out of her pocket, then fits it into the heavy lock on the chain-link gates. We help her drag the gates open. Deah gives me her cell number to call when we return.

"Thank you. I owe you, Deah."

"Repay me in knowledge," she says, "at a more convenient time for you. Now go."

I check out Ladd Street, which is a glorified alleyway with a few minor shop entrances. The coast is clear—only a single person walking away, with their back turned to us. It seems careless of Councilor Stone and her informants, if she knew we entered the Athenaeum; could they have given up on pursuing us so soon? Maybe she wasn't as threatened by me as I thought.

I give the signal to Nadia and Arreth, and the three of us dash across the street, entering the big municipal parking garage on its lowest level as Deah suggested. We cross through the dim space. Plenty of people are jockeying their cars into any remaining spaces and driving up to the upper levels of the garage, but none of them seem particularly interested in us. When we leave the garage on its north side and walk down Hanover Street, I glance back a few times, but I don't see anyone following us.

We take a long, circuitous path to my car, which I've parked over on leafy, residential Richards Ave at the end of Parrott, past the library. Arreth has been gazing curiously at her surroundings the whole time, noting the differences between this and her homeworld—more than the absence of humongous killer spiders, that is. As we reach my car, Arreth blurts out: "Who is your god here, if not Fath?"

"Ourselves, mostly," I say. "Money, for some."

She gives me a sharp, impatient look that is achingly familiar. "You know I'm not speaking metaphorically, Divya. Spare me."

I half-smile in return. "We don't—Arreth, not all of us are religious here. And those who are, they don't agree on one god. Some worship the Christian God... you may have noticed our North Church has a different symbol on top of the steeple than yours. I've never met my birth family, but I imagine they're Hindus—which is an umbrella name for a whole range of beliefs, most of them very different from Christianity. And..."

I stop, because I can see that Arreth looks completely lost. "Christianity?" she says. "Hindus?"

Nadia steps in. "Hey, I'm sorry, Divya. I wish I could've given you a primer on Fath worship before we left."

"Well, we don't have time to get edified," I say. "We've got to get to… you know who." I'm suddenly not so eager to drop Milly's name in front of Arreth, given how recently she lost her own version of the woman. Maybe I'll let the introduction speak for itself.

I jump in the driver's seat, and Nadia slides into shotgun; Arreth gets in the back. As I start the car, Nadia places a hand on the steering wheel.

"We had to move her," she says. "To a different safehouse —someone was poking around too close to the one you're familiar with. I'll show you the way."

I nod, frowning. It's hard to tell when Nadia's paranoia is vital, or just paranoia, but she's done a good job of keeping her Portwalkers a secret so far. Last I saw Milly was at a modest house near the water a block or so from the fish market in the South End, owned by a benefactor Nadia would not name. The potential spy could have been a nosy neighbor; there are plenty of those in the neighborhood. But, as I remember the cold hatred in Councilor Stone's face, I decide it'd be smart to adopt Nadia's level of caution from here on out.

Nada directs me out past the inlet with its impressive view of the derelict naval prison across the water, and on toward New Castle. We pass the little beach with its hidden Port leading to the bubble city of Stroyer's Axle, and then we go on to the island town itself.

I'm surprised at our destination. New Castle is a wealthy enclave, barely more than a village (in fact, the smallest town in the state), bristling with big houses enjoying water views on all sides—ninety-eight percent white and ninety percent Republican. It *would* be a great place to hide; the town values its privacy. Besides the Great Island Common park area, there are maybe three or four public parking spots on the whole island. But who could afford a hiding spot out here?

Nadia directs me down a private lane and into the driveway of a big house with a stunning view of the harbor and its various treasures: the Whaleback Light across the way at Fort Foster, the ramshackle structure on tiny Wood Island once known as a life-saving station, and the Portsmouth Harbor Lighthouse at the nearby Coast Guard station.

We climb out of the car and Arreth shades her eyes with her hand, looking out to sea. "Whose house is this?" she says.

"My parents'," Nadia answers.

∼

"Wait..." I say. "What?"

This is the first real bit of history I've learned about this mysterious woman heading the Portwalkers. I'd assumed, well, a more modest background—but I suppose, in retrospect, it makes sense. Wealthy conservative parents could indeed form a youth taking her rebellion all the way into other worlds, if only to draw a clear distinction between herself and Mom and Dad. But...

"Are Mr. and Mrs. Chopin *home*?" I ask, suddenly suspicious.

Nadia walks toward the rambling seaside manse. "No, they're dead," she says casually. "And their name wasn't Chopin. You always suspected it was a pseudonym, didn't you?"

I should have. We've got plenty of solid French names around these parts, including the one I received from my parents, but "Chopin" is rarely seen... "Fan of the composer, then?"

"Gotta love a good nocturne," Nadia says, grinning. "Come on, let's see our friends."

Arreth drags her feet behind us, her expression twisting as she examines the house. "Hey, girls... I know this place. In my world."

Nadia turns. The smile has faded from her face. "What? How?"

"Lord family lives here," says Arreth. "Ironic name for that family, too, because they're a big force in the local Reformed Temple, such as it is." When she sees our blank looks, she clarifies: "I guess I have to spell everything out with you people. The Reformers are—anti-magic. Splinter religion... they claim to worship Fath, but they don't call him the Giver. They think Fath doesn't want us to use our magic."

"I may be a Lord," Nadia says defensively, "but *I'm* not against your magic. I bet my parents would have been, though, if they lived in a world where magic existed."

"Jim and Phyllis Lord," Arreth says.

Now Nadia blanches. "Yes," she whispers.

Then, reluctantly, she asks: "What about... me? Over there?"

Arreth cocks her head. "*You* don't exist. The Lords only had a son. Never met him, but I'm sure he's as fanatical as his parents. Or, was... for all I know, they're all wiped out now by the fucking spiders."

Then she waves her hand impatiently and says, "If it's *not* a hotbed of anti-ability sentiment, then lead on, my friend. You're on a tight timeline, aren't you?"

"Yes, we are," I say. I can't help feeling satisfied that for once, Nadia's the one thrown for a loop by the alternate world.

Inside is an expansive space with plenty of pricy furniture and art objects, though many are dusty or damaged. Perhaps Nadia isn't as much of a careful curator as her parents were. I hear voices chatting in the kitchen, making me realize this is a haven for more than just Milly and her current "rehab" therapist, Durmaz 1N.

Nadia looks to me. "Ah, sounds like Donna and Airika are around. I don't think you've met them yet. Great folks." She adds at my look of alarm, "*Discreet* folks, too. We all have to be."

We head into the kitchen, where an older white woman with hippie-length grey hair is having iced tea with a young black woman. The latter's head is closely shaved; both are lean and fit. They could be a great advertisement for the legitimate side of the Tenacious Trainers. The guy in the corner, on the other hand, wouldn't make for a great poster. He looks up at us through thick black-rimmed glasses, his long and greasy hair falling in his face. He scratches at his prominent sideburns but says nothing, even as the two women greet us.

"Hey ladies," says Nadia, ignoring the guy, "is Milly home?"

"Out in the yard," the older woman says.

"Thanks, Donna." Nadia turns to the sideburns dude and adds, "Hey, Chola. Feet off the furniture."

He grudgingly complies. I realize now that he looks familiar, but I can't place where from...

"Did you say Milly?!" Arreth speaks up.

I know I shouldn't have put off explaining our plan to use an alternate version of her dead friend. I mean, duh. I open my mouth and say, "So, Arreth, when we saw—"

She's not listening, already on the move, running from the house. I follow her and see that she's circling around to the back, heading at great speed for the part of the property facing the ocean. Then she comes to a dead stop as she sees Milly and Durmaz iN.

The two of them are out on the lawn, apparently running some sort of practice or exercise for Milly. My eyeless friend is taking cautious steps around Adironack chairs arranged in a staggered line, like an obstacle course, while Durmaz encourages her forward. Milly has an apparatus strapped to her head that I didn't get to see last time I visited her; at the time, Durmaz was tweaking the tech, which he imported from his homeworld of Stroyer's Axle. As Durmaz spots Arreth, he draws a space-age weapon from his belt.

"Milly?" Arreth croaks, heedless of the man pointing a deadly silver... thing at her. "What happened to her *eyes,* goddammit? What kind of world is this?!" She takes a step forward.

"No closer!" Durmaz hollers.

"Whoa, whoa, whoa," I shout, hurrying to interpose myself in front of Arreth. "It's okay. What are you doing, Durmaz?"

"This woman is an impostor," he says. "No matter what she may have told you, Hannah Ryder died."

"Yes, I was *there*," I answer him bitterly. "I know."

Nadia belatedly shows up, waving her arms to pacify the otherworlder; only at the sight of her does he lower his weapon. "She's a friend," she barks at Durmaz.

"*That* remains to be seen," Arreth mutters.

"What's going on?" Milly asks. "Divya, Nadia, who's that with you?"

"It's gonna take a minute to explain," I say. I offer my

hand to Arreth. She slaps it away, looking furious, and maintains a distance from me as we approach Milly and Durmaz.

Up close, I see that Milly's helmet is topped with a little speaker and features large artificial ears that hook over her own. Durmaz had described it as an echolocation device. It uses ultrasonic frequencies that are then slowed and pitch-lowered to make them audible to human ears (and therefore useful for navigation). But he seemed confused when I referred to bats; somehow his people had replicated the wayfinding system bats use without having ever encountered the creatures. Indeed, now that I see it, the helmet's ears look like bat ears to me, triangular with curious ridges. *Pinnae,* I think Durmaz called them. The helmet makes Milly look ridiculous, but if it works, then I owe a debt of gratitude to Durmaz.

"What are you two doing out here, out in the open?" Nadia says—to Durmaz, not Milly.

She's right to be mad. The seaside houses are generously spaced on this street, but these two being outside, in full view of anyone on sea or land with a decent pair of binoculars, could be a significant security risk. Durmaz 1N shakes his head.

"I'm sorry," he says. "It didn't seem like any of the neighbors were around—everyone is down at Market Square Day—and Milly's been cooped up inside for so long. I thought we could get away with some outdoor practice."

"It was my idea," Milly says. "You don't have to take the blame."

"You can both take it," Nadia says coldly. "You're risking not only yourselves but the entire organization. Let's continue this conversation inside."

So it's left to me, as we walk back to the house, to fumblingly explain to both Arreth and Milly the information they're missing: where Arreth came from, what we would need Milly to do, and a brief recap of how Milly's eyes were stolen. When I'm finished, in the cool parlor of Nadia's late parents' house, Durmaz 1N says, "She's not ready. You can't put her in such a dangerous situation when she's not *ready* yet, Allard. She's gotten better at the manual echolocation—the mouth clicks—but I haven't finished calibrating the helmet."

"It's working fine, Durmaz," Milly puts in. "I only crashed into one lawn chair this time, and that was because we were interrupted."

"It's not up to me to decide," I say. "It's not up to you either, Durmaz. This is your choice, Milly... and I have to emphasize that none of us may make it back from New England-two. Between the trigger-happy military and the killer spiders, chances are not good."

"And this is all to save your clone," Milly says. "The one who killed four of my colleagues."

"Not *just* that," Arreth breaks in, eyeing Nadia. "They've also promised to stop the spiders."

"We said we'd see what we can do," I say. I rub my temple; it's so hard to think with this woman around. A constant mental struggle to see her as Arreth rather than you. And now we've got impossible task after impossible task piling up, and for all I know, they're cutting into Benazir's chest cavity down in Boston right now...

Someone squeezes my hand. Nadia has by now calmed herself about Durmaz and Milly's breach of protocol.

Milly frowns. "Sounds like a tall order."

"Lives are at stake," Arreth says. "You can't abandon us to the spiders—if you can't stop them, you need to provide us with a refuge. You people have all this room... and it's safe! I—"

"Hey, Arreth," Nadia breaks in, "why don't we let Milly and Divya talk. Let's go upstairs. You're looking pretty rough; I bet some of Donna's clothes would fit you."

She stands and indicates the foyer, wearing a gentle but firm expression. Arreth's eyes dart from Milly to me, then she loudly sighs and gets up to follow Nadia out. Durmaz ɪN lingers, feeling responsibility for his "patient" in the face of unreasonable demands, but he does us the courtesy of ambling to the other side of the room. Sunlight slants through the windows, as if beckoning us back outside.

Milly says, "I quit, you know. Talked to Akerman on the phone, so he wouldn't have to see... this. Turns out he was ready to fire me anyway after I went AWOL and couldn't provide a good reason for it."

"You don't have to keep their secrets," I say, nodding in Durmaz's direction, using him as shorthand for the cult itself.

Milly snorts. "What am I supposed to do, turn these people in? After what they've done for me?"

"It doesn't have to cost you *everything*. You stumbled into this mess of the Ports and the Portwalkers... even Durmaz helping you out doesn't obligate you to take their side. There are still good cops on the force, like McLaren and Haring." I hesitate. "I... hate to see another good one hang up her badge."

Milly's hands tighten, seek each other. She weaves her fingers together. "What am I supposed to do, become a dispatcher? No, Divya. Even with the help of this helmet, my days on the streets are done. There's no way. You keep framing things as a choice for me, when you know very well that they aren't choices at all. Like this suicide mission you lay at my feet."

"So it's not a choice," I say. "There's no way you can do it."

"No, you idiot, there's no way I *can't*." Her lips curl into a grimace. "If someone needs my help, if it's a matter of life and death, then there's no way I can refuse, no matter how dangerous it might be. And you knew that about me before you walked in here."

The eternal protector, even without her badge. Yes—I may not have wanted to admit it to myself, but I knew. I search for what to say and come up empty.

"I know that about you, too," she adds in a quieter, less hostile voice. "Ah, Allard. How did we get ourselves to this point? And how do we get out?"

I think about the ruined, desperate world that I'm going to lead her to.

"There's blood along any path we take," I say. "All we can do is hope that a minimum of it is ours."

6

Before we leave the Lord house and New Castle, I make a call to Ethan Jeong.

"Divya?" he says. I can hear the roar of Boston summer traffic in the background. "How are you calling me?"

"We're off schedule," I say. "I'm back in our world."

"What?! Why?"

I give him a brief rundown of what's happened. "Find a way to postpone Benazir's—operation. For at least a day."

To his credit, Jeong didn't interrupt me once while I was talking about Portsmouth$_2$. But now he lets all of his frustration and anger pour out: "Dammit. *Dammit!* I can't march in there and start ordering around ASACs, Allard. I'm only an SSA—an acting SSA under investigation—and this whole operation depended on subtlety. And Harriman's only going to help me as long as I don't put him at risk. If I show that I need her to stay alive, they're going to get suspicious. What am—"

"You have to think of something," I say. "I'm not sure we can even drive on the highways in New England-two. If we have to get down to Boston-two on, like, fucking horseback, then it'll take a long time to get to the FBI office-two."

"Stop saying 'two.' Why do you keep saying that?" A horn blares somewhere near Jeong.

"It keeps that world, those people, *separate* in my head. Believe me, if you went there, you'd have to be doing constant mental gymnastics too."

"Oh, sorry, that's right, I've got the easy job of breaking someone out of a federal facility." But then his tone softens. "Allard, are you *sure* you want to do this? This other world sounds like it's going to kill you."

"Yes."

"And all this for a psychopathic killer who happens to wear your face."

"Whatever she's done, she doesn't deserve what your people have planned. But if you're trying to get out of this, I understand."

All I hear is random snatches of music, a shout, someone laughing, and the ever-present whoosh of a thousand mobile polluters. Then Jeong says, "I'm not backing out. You saved my life in Avariccia. I'll never forget that."

After another pause, he says, "I'm about to do my interview with Benazir about World 72—when I'm done, I'll tell them I need to do a follow-up interview tomorrow morning. Harriman will back me up. Marsters and her clones are his case, and obviously they connect to World 72 as well. The two of us together could make a strong argument to Ivanov for squeezing some final information from Benazir before she's... no longer able to speak."

I doubt Benazir will remember anything about Graham's World, a.k.a. World 72—she only came into being when I returned *from* that world. But I say, "Do it. We'll get down to Boston-two—the other Boston—as soon as we can and then send you a signal through Nadia's Compass." I hesitate. "We're bring Milly Fragonard along."

"Milly? Why?!"

"It's hard to explain. But she's a willing participant, and we'll take care of her."

"Can I talk to her?"

"I..." I cut off my own objection. I don't want to make decisions for Milly. "Sure, let me get her."

I find Milly and hand the phone over. Then I leave the room, giving her privacy for the conversation. I'd like to think there's something special between Ethan and Milly. That there could be sparks there someday, given the right fuse, even taking her disfigurement into account.

The Portwalkers see us off from the covered front porch of the Lord house. Airika and Donna have their companionable arms around each other. The sideburns hipster, Chola, smokes a cigarette and waves. I remember now where I've seen him before—he's the drummer for the Hairless Werewolves. You would ask for his autograph. They're your favorite local band. I'm wondering if the other band members are in the cult, too.

Durmaz IN glowers at me for putting his patient at risk. Or maybe it's for putting the echolocation helmet at risk; hard to say. On my advice, Milly takes the helmet off and puts on an oversized pair of sunglasses borrowed from Nadia, in case someone spots her in the car. Nadia glances back at the house as I drive away, thinking secret thoughts.

Arreth, for her part, continues to gawk out the window. I half-expect her to jump out of the car and run off before we can return her to her nightmare homeworld. But, no, she was a nurse there like you were here, and she refrains from abandoning her people. She sticks with our group as we park near downtown Portsmouth, again in a tucked-away spot.

As Milly climbs out, I say to her loudly, "Need a hand?"

She shakes her head. "I gotta do this on my own. And I hear you fine."

She removes her shades and straps on the echolocation helmet. I watch, apprehensive, as her feet approach the curb —and she steps up without incident. *Thank you, Durmaz...*

We creep back through the parking garage, Milly bringing up the rear, moving slowly and cautiously. I look back at her, but she's doing fine avoiding the parked cars. As a truck rolls down the ramped floor toward us, she murmurs, "Watch out," and goes between two parked vehicles until the truck passes.

"Hey," I say, "that was great. You saw it coming."

"Heard it," she corrects. "Before I sensed it, even."

She takes the helmet back off, stashing it in her bag, and replaces the shades on her face before we leave the cover of the garage. I dial Deah Sloane and give her the heads up that we're back and need the gates reopened. I watch for the sight of the librarian pulling at a high gate, and then I lead the four of us across Ladd Street.

As we approach the gates, I hear a man shout, "Hey! Stop!"

Shit. I know that voice.

"Go, go," I order my companions, waving frantically at the gate. "Get through and close that fucking gate."

Arreth and Milly don't hesitate to obey. Nadia, however, lingers too long—she's with me as the cop and councilor show up. And neither Deah nor the others make a move to close the gate without us. Damn.

Officer Leon Gomez has his Sig Sauer P226 drawn on us as he approaches, with Councilor Jack Wegman close behind him. Neither of them seem worried about causing a scene—conveniently, there aren't any pedestrians in the alley-street. I wonder, belatedly, if their colleagues had something to do with that. We've skulked right into their trap.

"Help you, Leon?" I ask innocently. I make like I'm perfectly comfortable staring into the blackness of his gun barrel.

"Get on your knees, girl," he says. "Same with the rest of you. Hands in the air."

I'd prefer not to take such an order from a man. But he barks "*Now!*" and the others comply, and I remember this is one of the crooked cops who didn't hesitate to kill Portwalkers when they got too inconvenient. They haven't made the charges stick yet, unlike with Mike Prince, but I know Gomez—he probably did do it. I get on the ground too. Gomez reaches behind me and grabs my Glock from my waistband. He throws the gun into the courtyard.

"What are the charges, officer?" I ask his shoes.

"Death threat," he says. "You haven't forgotten already, have you? That was this morning."

"I thought Grace Stone wasn't scared of me."

Now Councilor Wegman joins the conversation. "Order must be upheld in this city. Fear has nothing to do with it."

"Pah," I say. But now both of them are looking at Milly Fragonard, Gomez with his mouth agape.

"Milly," he says in a low voice. "What the fuck are you doing with these lowlifes? *This* is why you left the PD?"

I see sweat trickling down Milly's face. Her sunglasses are sliding down her nose, and she can't fix them with her hands up. She wrinkles her nose several times, frantically trying to move the shades back up. "No, it was because I couldn't stand your B.O. anymore," she says. "Ask Rick sometime what it's like to be stuck in a cruiser with you... you're not going to like the answer."

Officer Gomez takes a few quick steps toward her, switching his aim from my head to hers, but Wegman says, "Hey. Gomez. Try to focus here. Get cuffs on 'em and bring 'em all in—without bruises, or Grace is going to have words."

"How many fucking handcuffs do you think I have?"

"Start with Allard, she's the instigator."

Gomez glares at Wegman. "I'll start with who I want, and I don't care what your bitch-ass says. Fragonard is twice the size of the dyke."

Once we're in their custody, we're toast. Have to think. Something tickles the back of my mind about Jack Wegman. I blurt, "Last I saw you, you were digging through the rubble. You were a heartburner."

He shoots me a confused look. "Huh? Enough of your nonsense. Gomez, I'm telling you, cuff *Allard* first."

"I'm not afraid of that little bitch."

"But you are afraid of Milly?" I say to Gomez.

He snorts angrily and grabs Milly's wrists, pulling them together while keeping his gun practically jammed up against her forehead. His rough handling jostles the sunglasses on Milly's face, and they slide right off, revealing the smooth flesh where her eyes should be.

"What the *fuck*?!" Gomez cries out. He staggers back from her, the gun loosening in his hand, practically about to trip over Arreth.

And Arreth—well, she has all of your impulsiveness and the same lack of common sense. She seizes the opportunity and one of her raised hands snatches the pistol out of Gomez's grasp.

Good girl.

Gomez whirls to her in surprise. He doesn't know her, because he didn't know you. So unlike with Milly, there's nothing to be shocked about. Just fury at having his toy stolen. But he's not a complete idiot, so he starts to raise his own hands, even as he says, "Give—"

Arreth fires. The shot enters Leon Gomez's head from under his chin and exits through his cranium.

The mess is sudden, and horrible.

She vaults to her feet as Gomez is falling, his brain tissue dripping from the chain links of the gate. Her hands are shaking as she swings the P226 toward Wegman next.

"*No!*" I shout. "No! Arreth, *stop!*"

She stops. I'm on my feet but I dare not get too close. Wegman's eyes are bugging out of his head at the corpse that was Gomez. I don't think he even realizes that Arreth is targeting him. Nadia and Milly and Deah Sloane are still on the ground, two of them looking at Arreth in horror, the third darting her head around and asking, "What happened? What happened?"

"Gomez is dead," I answer her. I banish the shakiness from my voice, forcing myself to take control of the situation. "And Councilor Wegman could be next, but he doesn't have to be if he cooperates with us. I-isn't that right, Jack?"

"You are in *deep shit,* all of you," the city councilor says, finally coming back into focus. But he raises his hands, slowly, as he speaks.

"I didn't mean to do it," Arreth says, in a dull voice entirely unlike her (well, *you*).

"We're past intent," I say harshly. "Gomez can't hear you."

Not that I'm mourning the murderous bastard, but this puts a significant wrinkle in our mission. Sure, we can march right into the Athenaeum now, but will we ever be able to come *back*?

"We need to handle him," Nadia says, getting to her feet. "He saw what Arreth did, saw all of us." She offers a hand to Milly, who grasps it and gets up as well.

"And what do you suggest?" I ask.

Nadia nods at dead Gomez. "These are not good people, Divya."

Jeong dropped a similar suggestion when we returned from the City of Games with another "not-good" councilor in tow, Sandy Grieg. Then, as now, I refused to become like our enemies for the sake of convenience. I'd expected ruthlessness from a federal agent like Jeong, but to see Nadia offer a similar suggestion... it hurts.

"*No*," I snap at her. "What the fuck is wrong with you?"

"Can I say," puts in Milly, "that I didn't sign onto this to be a party to murder either. *How,* exactly, did your friend wind up blowing away Gomez?"

"It just *happened*," Arreth insists. "Milly, I know that cop in my world. He's one of the worst... or was. Pretty sure the last spider attack got him. But still."

This new argument is incompatible with Arreth's last one—that she didn't mean to do it. But I don't have the luxury of prying into her psyche right now. I look over at the librarian, who has gotten up from the ground but otherwise hasn't moved much. "Deah, you have any rope in the Athenaeum? Anything to tie someone up with?"

"It's a library, not a fetish shop," Deah Sloane answers tartly. Her arms are crossed over her chest, as if she's hugging herself, and her eyes are wide and scared, fixed on Arreth. Of course she doesn't dare to move—she thinks she could be the next victim.

Sorry. "You, get into the courtyard," I say to the city councilor. "Milly, Nadia, close the gates."

Nadia glances down. "Divya, we've got a... blockage."

"Drag *him* in, then do it," I say, boiling into a fury. I notice that Councilor Wegman hasn't moved. "Get a fucking move on, Jack, or the loose cannon'll fire again!"

Reluctantly the councilor shuffles into the courtyard, stepping over the body of the crooked cop. Nadia wrinkles her nose and bends to pull Gomez's body away from the radii of the gates; once it's clear, she and Milly close the gates. Nadia plucks the gate lock from the unresisting hand of Deah Sloane, who still looks shocked and fearful. I can't blame her for not knowing who the good guys are, after seeing what Arreth did. I'm having a doubt or two myself.

"So," Wegman asks, "what are you going to do with me?"

Showing mercy to him won't score points with Councilor Stone. I know we're past that threshold. But maybe Wegman could become an asset rather than a liability.

"You're going to wait here until your buddies show up," I say. "Then you're gonna give them a report that leaves us out of it altogether. Officer Gomez went rogue, threatened a poor defenseless librarian, and *you* were forced to kill him in self-defense."

"Why the *fuck* would I tell them that?" Wegman says, his mouth dangling open.

"Because when we're done with our—errand," I say, "we'll help you find your missing daughter. The Book and Bar could use her back behind the bar anyway."

"*What?!*" Nadia says in almost a shriek. "No *way*. No way am I helping any councilor with *anything*, not after all they've done. And especially not regarding Valerie. She's much safer—"

She claps a hand over her mouth, realizing she's given away too much.

Jack Wegman looks at her, the hate and fear draining out of his eyes as hope seeps in. "You know her," he says, speaking faster. "You know Valerie... She's still alive? You know she's alive and where she is?"

Nadia's face is pale and tight with anger. "Divya, a word in private?"

We take a few steps away, leaving Arreth to guard Wegman with the P226. Nadia whispers, "Goddammit, Divya. Valerie Wegman wanted to escape her father. Her boyfriend Judah was one of my Portwalkers—she went through a Port with him. I don't think she *wants* to come back."

"What if there's a chance, however slim, that we could get Wegman on our side? Think of the trouble that's waiting for us when we come back from the other world. Wegman knows your face now, Nadia. He could match notes with Councilor Stone and figure out who you are."

She simmers. "And you think making him this ludicrous offer is easier, somehow, than putting a bullet in his head."

"Who's going to fire the bullet?" I ask. "I saw your reaction when Arreth shot Gomez. You're not a killer, Nadia, no matter how much you hate the city councilors."

She rolls her eyes and looks away from me.

"I said we could help him find his daughter. I didn't say anything about surrendering Val to him. We could arrange a simple meeting, with all the power on our side, so there's no way he can kidnap her back." I pause. "You *do* know where she is, don't you?"

Nadia shrugs, but I can read her body language. Yes.

Finally she says, "You don't always have to be so goddamn *rational*. Before I met you, I thought *you* were supposed to be the loose cannon... I should've listened to Hannah."

We return to Wegman. He looks from me to Arreth with her Sig P226.

"Okay," he says. "You don't shoot me, and I'll go with your cover story. Maybe Deah here will even play along. Won't you, Deah?"

The librarian grimaces at him but says nothing.

"You'd *better* keep your promise," Wegman says to me. "I need to see Valerie again."

"It's a deal," I say.

Arreth looks perplexed. "You trust him?"

"He's got something to lose," I say, "just like the rest of us."

She lowers the pistol. Councilor Wegman confers with Deah in a low voice. I go looking for the Glock 26 I lost and find it underneath a parked car.

I jab the button to the glass elevator. "I'll save you some steps, Milly—come in the elevator with me. Nadia and Arreth, take the stairs, please."

It's close quarters inside the elevator cab. As we ascend, Milly takes her helmet out of her bag and fumbles it onto her head, and I watch the courtyard. Wegman seems to be pleading with Deah. She holds up her palm to his face in a universal gesture and gets out her phone. I can't fault her if she's decided not to corroborate Wegman's story. But if she does implicate us, it'll be the final nail in our coffin... I don't know how we'll return to Portsmouth without facing immediate arrest. The Athenaeum is a trap.

Maybe Portsmouth$_2$ will grow on you. That's your voice in my head, darkly amused, and I snort.

"See something funny?" Milly asks. "Tell me there's something funny in all this."

"You hear the one about the chicken that crossed the Port?" I answer her. The elevator door slides open on the library floor.

I hear a faint and unwelcome sound, growing stronger. Sirens. "Let's hurry," I say.

7

Nadia and Arreth emerge from the stairwell; we only beat them by a hair. The four of us go through the library and enter the exhibit room. The wall where the Port is concealed looks different than before, to my eye: wrinkled, and I could swear one of the framed pictures didn't have a crack in the glass before.

Arreth dares another look out the window while Nadia opens the Port. "Lot of cops out there right now, clearing a path through the crowd," Arreth says.

"They'll be coming through the back too," I say.

Milly cocks her head. "I told myself I'd never go through one of these things again."

"I'm sorry," I tell her, and I am. It wasn't long ago that I came to *her* rescue—and now am I going to throw her life away in a different world? For a vicious little shit? "I'll be with you the whole time."

"Well, I won't need someone to hold my hand," she answers. "Only... tell me if I'm about to get hit by a car."

The wind from the Port sighs through my hair, tickling the black strands that have come loose from my hair tie. I brace myself for what's to come, glancing at the door—it'd be nice to go through a Port without someone hot on my heels. But I don't hear anyone yet... maybe Gomez's body is providing a sufficient distraction.

Nadia stops moving, stops muttering her incantation, and flings the last handful of feathers at the Port. It shivers to its full diameter, the ruined Athenaeum visible beyond. Nobody's peeking back at us, which is a hopeful sign. Nadia steps through the Port. Arreth glances at Milly and me, then back at the Port; she grits her teeth, shaking her head, and goes through next.

"It's open?" Milly asks.

"Yeah," I say. "Can you... feel it?"

"Yeah." Fear traces its way across her features, and my heart lurches.

"You don't have to go," I say in a spasm of regret.

"The hell I don't." Again, that bitter twist to her voice, reminding me I've locked her into a cage built of her own integrity.

"After you, then."

I watch her walk uncertainly toward the Port. She places her right arm through first. "I forgot how it... huh."

Now they're entering the building; I can hear them. I sigh and push Milly through the rest of the way, following close behind. She gasps in surprise. For the briefest instant both of us are in that not-space together, linked by physical contact, and the tingling in my body jangles more unpleasantly than usual, as if set off by the reaction in Milly's own body.

Then we're through, and I lead Milly a safe distance away from the Port, nodding at Nadia. "Close it off quick."

Nadia does.

Milly steps gingerly over the scattered debris on the exhibit room floor. "Spiders, you said?"

"Big ones," Arreth agrees. She steps to the open wall and then skitters backward, waving frantically at the rest of us. "Oh, shit. *Stay back*."

That's the drawback to having a whole wall's worth of real estate as one's window. If anyone looks up at this floor of the Athenaeum$_2$, they'll be able to see us. I flatten against one crumbling side wall and try to get a better look down at Market Square$_2$.

Yep. It's crawling with sailors. Now that they've taken over the Eostrix, they're commandeering the rest of the downtown as part of their outpost as well. A ragged man harangues them from atop a pile of rubble: it's Wegman$_2$. One of the sailors fires at him, almost casually, and Wegman$_2$ falls. I see a group of women gathered at gunpoint near the remains of the North Church—

Church of "Fath?"

—and I have a sick feeling about what the sailors have in store for them.

"What did you say?" Milly speaks up.

"What did I say? Uh, nothing..." I retreat from my vantage point. "No one else said anything, either."

"Hmm." Milly furrows her brow and lets the topic drop.

"There's no freaking way we're gonna get past all those sailors," Arreth says. "We should use the back exit, like we did in your world."

I recall what I glimpsed the last time I was here: the rubble piled up at the back of the Athenaeum$_2$, the glass elevator smashed. "I think it's blocked. Not gonna be an option."

"Fath damn it all."

"What if you could use your... dollar magic somehow, to

help us?" Nadia asks her. "You can see into the future, right?"

"No, only into the *past,* remember?" Arreth says. "A.k.a. the dead and buried. Don't see how that'll help."

Yep, that's why Nadia calls it dollar magic. Next to worthless. I think through alternate plans. "Wish we didn't stick out so much."

I look at the remains of the Athenaeum$_2$ exhibit—the *historical* exhibit—and then it hits me. Even with the models and maps and artifacts smashed, I can tell the exhibit has the same theme as the one back at our Athenaeum. "Wait a minute." I go over to where I remember the World War II naval uniforms on display in our world.

They're buried in junk and ripped and dirty. They might do the trick, though. With some help from Arreth digging through the rubble, I pluck out three serviceable uniforms. They're odd-looking—one of the uniforms involves shorts and long white socks—but they do resemble modern-day service dress whites. At a distance.

Nadia has a strange look on her face as she looks at Arreth and me hoisting our prizes.

"There's only three," she points out.

"None of them are big enough to fit Milly anyway," I say. "She'll have to be our 'prisoner.'"

"But they think they already killed Milly." Arreth adds. "They won't appreciate her coming back from the dead."

Milly taps her echolocation helmet. "They won't recognize me while I have this on."

I slip into the uniform closest to my size, the one with the shorts and long socks. I feel silly, though I don't look much sillier than either Arreth or Nadia in their own forties-era uniforms. Arreth sneaks another glance through the open wall, and then the four of us proceed downstairs.

As we emerge from the wrecked reading room onto Congress Street, Arreth holds Gomez's pistol against Milly's broad back. We, the proud all-female reenactors of past wars, attract little notice from the real sailors. Most of them are focused on moving supplies around and rounding up civilians, either to be held prisoner like the women or summarily executed at the first sign of resistance.

How quickly did they slide into brutality? It couldn't have taken long, given the timeline of the spider attacks. What might happen in my own world if and when monstrous beasts are unleashed there?

Then Milly loses her footing.

I'm not sure what it was: a piece of rubble or wire, or a hole in the brick walk. But Milly's gadgetry fails her for a second, and it's enough to send her sprawling, with an unwilling cry of dismay. Her helmet flies from her head. Nadia dives for the helmet. Multiple sailors turn their heads.

One is the sailor who conjured the illusion of the spider outside the Eostrix's windows. The guy recognizes her as the troublemaker that his commanding officer confronted earlier. The woman who's supposed to be dead from a wound to the neck.

Fuck.

The sailor cries out to his nearby comrades. Pistols and Mossbergs swing in our direction. Arreth freezes in the middle of helping Milly back up, and Nadia abandons the helmet and raises her hands. I stay where I am, but I don't bother to put up my own hands this time.

The sailor—mindfucker, they called him—hisses an order to a subordinate, who goes running off, presumably to fetch Command Master Chief Brooks. Then he takes a cautious step toward us. "The woman from the Eostrix?

How is this possible? And what happened to her eyes, Fath damn it?!"

"Maybe you fucked with the wrong people," Arreth spits at him. "Murderer."

Then she pauses, realizing the same label could apply to her.

The mindfucker frowns at her. "Oh, and I remember you. Nice outfit. Wrong war."

"What are you calling this new war?" I ask him.

"Soon as we find out which fucking terrorist group set these spiders on us, I'll let you know. Command Master Chief!"

This last yell was directed at the man approaching them at a brisk walk, the soft-featured killer in charge of these sailors. Brooks can't contain his surprise at seeing Milly, though he does his best to stay cool and professional.

"You won't stay down, it seems," he observes.

"He talking to me?" Milly asks.

"There's more to this than you'll ever understand," I say to Brooks. "Why don't you let us go and we'll be out of your hair for good."

"No," Arreth cuts in bravely, stupidly. "*I'll* be back for the survivors, if you've left any, you damn monster."

Brooks eyes her as if a mosquito on his white sleeve has begun talking to him. "The facility is the property of the United States government. Your former patients are under our care, and you are prohibited from the area. This is a matter of national security."

She stares at him, hard. Then her eyes unfocus, and the air shimmers around her.

"You had better *not*," the command master chief says, raising his hand toward her. I'm not sure exactly why, but I instantly feel crippling discouragement wash over me.

What are we even doing here? Why are we even trying?

Arreth's gaze sharpens. "A blond man, wide shoulders," she says. "I know him. Bill Sommers. You shot him, two minutes ago."

"I told you not to do that," Brooks snarls. His hand makes a twisting motion.

Now Arreth frowns and droops her head. "Not... that it matters," she says, in a glummer tone, "but I saw the woman you let your men drag off, too. For 'comfort,' you said."

"Arreth," Milly says, and she sounds startled. "He's sending a wave of something toward you—toward us. I can *see* it. Resist it."

"Heartburner," Nadia mutters. "Right."

A wave of discouragement, I realize, and it must be spilling onto me too. I make an extra effort to overcome my drop in spirits; it's easier to do so now that I know it's not coming from me.

"You can *see* what I'm doing?" Brooks asks. "You've got even more talents than I realized. Yes, you'd definitely be an asset to the Navy. Alive, that is, so please don't make us kill you again." He pauses. "How *did* you recover from that neck wound so quickly? Did a creep heal you?"

"I'm not who you think I am," Milly says. Then she winces. "Divya? They're coming."

"Who's coming?" I ask.

"It's..." She trails off. Her face crumples in revulsion. "They're chittering, but it's *words*—not that they have much to say. But they're hungry. They keep talking about something called 'Bloated Belly?' And they're *coming*. They'll be here soon."

At the mention of "Bloated Belly," Nadia pales and says, "Fuck. So it is that one."

"*What* one? What?" Arreth snaps. Her black cloud of

hair trembles as she looks from Nadia to Milly to me. "Is it the spiders? Are the spiders coming back?!"

"They want to eat us," Milly says. "No, eat our *tides*, whatever that means. Yeah, they're coming back all right—"

"She can hear them!" the mindfucker sailor says. His gun wavers. "The rumors were true."

"Or it's a delaying tactic," CMDCM Brooks says. "Don't be so quick to—"

"I'm serious," Milly says angrily. "We all need to get out of Portsmouth *now*."

"But if they're after our tides," Nadia muses aloud, "they'll follow us."

"Be quiet, all of you!" Brooks roars. The note of panic in his voice is plain to hear. "Shut your goddamn mouths. *I* decide our next move."

But now *I'm* picking up on something that the rest of them can't detect. Not the spiders, though I'm sure straight-and-narrow Milly is telling the truth about *them*. No, this is the sound of many new footsteps approaching, human footsteps. The cavalry come to save us, or more sailors to back up Brooks?

I strain to listen. I catch the faintest trace of voices snapping at each other: "Major Wade, I…"

Major. That's not a Navy rank. But it is one in, among other branches, the *Air Force*—I'm betting it's a contingent from the Pease airbase. Could provide a useful distraction if they're not planning on shooting us too. Will they get here before the spiders do? Before Brooks marches us off to our deaths? Well, except for Milly, who he's planning on keeping around as a pet.

Brooks is off balance. I might push him too far and get a bullet as thanks, but if I can keep him teetering…

"Command Master Chief," I say loudly, "what's your plan to fight the spiders?"

He whips back toward me. "Didn't I tell you bitches to shut up?"

"I'm sorry." *Fill his bucket,* my therapist would say. *Fill it to the brim.* "Sir. I'm scared. We're all scared, and we could use some reassurance, sir. Do you know anything about where the spiders came from, how they happened?"

"Divya, we *don't have time for this*," Milly hisses at me. Inadvertently, she's making the fear angle convincing. I wish she could trust me, for once, that I know what I'm doing.

"Please, Command Master Chief," I say.

The march of boots draws closer. As does the burrowing of mutant spiders.

CMDCM Brooks hasn't softened, exactly. But my appeal to his military machismo—*oh please save us little ladies, sir!*—has changed his stance; now he's puffing out his chest as he responds. "Any specific information about the macrobiological threat is, of course, classified," he says to me. "But it seems clear to me that a chemical agent from a hostile actor must have aggravated the growth of normal insects into monsters. Whether that hostile actor is a foreign nation such as Russia or a terrorist group such as—"

"Arachnids," Arreth says.

"What?" The command master chief's nostrils flare.

"Spiders are arachnids, not insects," Arreth says.

So she's determined to get us all killed, I see. My bucket-filling strategy sinks underneath a flood of anger. I turn to her. "You dumb shit!" I snarl. "Why do you *always* have to have the last word?"

She gapes at me with a painfully familiar expression of wounded innocence. "The fuck are you saying? You don't know me!"

Now CMDCM Brooks unholsters his own weapon. "I *told* you to—"

"Command Master Chief!" calls out a sailor at the perimeter of the group. "Air Force, inbound."

From the stormy look on his face, Brooks wants to shoot us all and *then* deal with the newcomers. Take one problem at a time. But enough of his ragged discipline remains for him to spit out an oath and snap at the mindfucker sailor: "*Hold them here.* If any of them move, including the spider-whisperer, shoot them all. I'll be back shortly."

We can all see the Air Force men approaching now, maintaining a rough formation as they climb over the rubble, approaching from the direction of Maplewood Avenue. They're on foot, as my sensitive ears detected—why not a tank, or at least a motorcycle or two? Brooks meets their leader, and I can hear every word of the conversation that unfolds:

Brooks: "Wade."

Wade: "Major Wade, to you. We're commandeering the downtown; from here on you'll be answering to me."

Brooks: "Fuck that. I don't answer to any flyboy."

Wade: "Do you see these fucking stripes, Brooks? I outrank you."

Brooks: "The day the Navy takes orders from the Air Force—"

Wade: "Listen up, squid. We all answer to the Pentagon, or have you forgotten?"

Brooks: "Have *you* heard from the Pentagon lately? Because I fucking haven't. For all we know, it's a crater by now. Like your airbase."

Wade: "I've been getting disturbing reports about the way you're handling things downtown. So, you know what? I don't care if the Joint Chiefs are bones in the ground. I'm taking over here. CMDCM Brooks, you are relieved of duty. You—"

My concentration is interrupted by a croak from Milly: "Divya. *We have to go, now.*"

I look at her. She hasn't dared move toward me under gunpoint, or move at all, but her whole body is tensed. I feel like I'm picking up minute vibrations from the street now as well.

I glance at the mindfucker sailor and see the terror on his face. He believes every word Milly's saying. Good.

"If you stay here," I tell him, "you're committing suicide."

He stares at me and then gives me a tiny, mute nod.

"Your insane commanding officer is a dead man," I say, now addressing the rest of the sailors keeping us captive. "He's going to stay here until one of those monsters eats him alive. But none of you have to stay. Look—" I gesture at Brooks and Wade, who have devolved into a shouting match. "—this is our chance. We can all get out of here. But we need to do it *NOW*."

I practically shout the last word. It acts as a spell-breaker on the mindfucker and the others, who all lower their weapons and scatter. But I'm not going to pat myself on the back too much, because now we can all feel the tremors underneath us. Even Brooks and Wade hesitate in their argument.

They look over, but it's too late—us four mouthy "bitches" are already running for cover, Nadia seizing Milly's hand to give her guidance. I find myself in the lead. I automatically steer us in the direction we've been neglecting to go all this time: south. Toward Pleasant Street, which is looking anything but.

We haven't cleared downtown when the first monsters burst through the ground around us.

8

Like the Portsmouth I know, Portsmouth$_2$ is a small city, a jumped-up town. A car can drive through the downtown in a minute or two. However, on foot, especially when under attack from gigantic burrowing monsters, a visitor to Portsmouth$_2$ may find the distance from block to block stretches out to infinity.

I'm not far down Pleasant Street$_2$, if that's what it's called here (street signs have been smashed to oblivion). I've passed the spot where my apartment would be in my world —the upper floors of the building here are in ruin—and I'm coming up to the intersection with Court Street$_2$ when the constant rumbling under my feet turns into explosions. Behind me, in front of me, on Court$_2$ in both directions, bricks and ragged pieces of asphalt punch outward in a ring around each of the spiders surfacing.

I hit the ground to avoid projectiles, arms over my head, and look up at the nearest spider.

It is, as I expected, the stuff of nightmares: a bouquet of stiff, hairy legs splaying out around a shaggy head riddled with obsidian eyes and crowned by pincers the size of snowplow blades. From somewhere underneath the pincers I hear a screeching noise. *Milly can interpret that?*

I hear screams all around me. Most of them are male: a good number of the sailors fled in the same direction I chose. For whatever reason, the several spiders emerging from the ground are targeting the Navy guys first, whipping out their multi-jointed legs and curling around their victims to haul them toward the pincers.

Gunshots to my left. I see the mindfucker sailor emptying his clip at the appendage approaching him. But even a few slugs embedding in that leg—about as big around as a young tree—don't stop it from squeezing him between its joints. His bones break audibly and his tormented shriek is endless as the spider lifts him toward its mouth.

"*Divya!*"

Milly is dusty but alive, sprawled over a heap of broken street near me. I barrel toward her and help her to her feet. Curiously, though her head isn't injured—she is, after all, wearing a *helmet*—she's got both hands clapped to her skull. Not over her ears or the bat pinnae attached to them, but on her temples. "God-*dang* this chatter!" she yells in my ear, far louder than she needs to.

I grab her shoulders and rotate her in the right direction to clear Court Street without running straight into a spider or a sinkhole. "Go!" I yell. "Run straight! I'll be with you in a minute!"

"But—"

"Do it!"

Milly takes off at a healthy run, jerking as her helmet directs her to avoid obstacles on the road. Most of the debris she can simply jump over with enough speed built up. I spin to locate the others. Nadia's running toward me, sailors falling and dying to the spiders behind her—she's scraped up but doing fine—but Arreth...

Fath dammit!

One spider has taken a shine to Arreth, who's crumpled on the ground, holding one of her legs—some flying fragment bloodied it or worse. She's in enough pain not to notice the house-sized creature hefting itself out of its hole to fling its legs at her.

"Arreth!" I scream. I saw how futile the mindfucker's bullets were against the spiders, but I still grab my gun and shoot at the monster's legs approaching her. Maybe it'll be enough to distract the thing, at least...

To find a different meal? You sneer in my mind, apparently indifferent to the fate of your alternate self.

The legs do stop advancing for a second when my rounds rip into them. They flutter as the spider swivels its head and its black eyes take me in. But I must be less tantalizing of a target than Arreth, because the spider turns back to her and snakes a leg around her as she's struggling to her feet.

Nadia surges past me and flings out both hands toward Arreth, screaming incoherently. I blink—suddenly there are *multiple* Arreths in the small space encircled by the spider's leg. All with an injured leg, all grimacing. The spider hesitates, seeming confused. An Arreth moves to escape. The spider closes its leg around the other seven or eight Arreths as the escaping one hobbles toward me, wide-eyed.

"Grab her on one side, I'll grab the other," Nadia yells at me. "We need to get her clear of this area—hurry!"

Nadia and I support Arreth, who's gritting her teeth in pain but is clearly glad to see us. The next several seconds are a blur of urgency and motion as we try to move as quickly as possible past the perimeter of spider holes. I glimpse more sailors running forward, trying to rescue their friends, dying. Command Master Chief Brooks must be sending in fresh troops.

Milly rushes toward us, recognizing our voices, but I wave her off. "South," I say. "South toward the mill pond."

The four of us make our unsteady way across the land bridge bisecting the South Mill Pond, toward Portsmouth$_2$'s municipal complex, which—if it weren't wrecked by underground invaders—would closely resemble the one back in my own Portsmouth except for the carved eye statues that adorn the top of the crumbling police station.

As we head up the hill in the direction of the complex, another mammoth-sized spider bursts from the ground back on the other side of the pond. It climbs out of its hole, waving its many legs (far more than eight) and swiveling its head. We stop, tensed for another attack, but the spider skitters toward the downtown instead.

"More tides to consume there," Nadia muses aloud. "More people gathered together. We'll want to avoid crowds."

"Wait, what?" I ask.

"How much farther are we going?" Arreth groans. "My leg is on fucking *fire*." She shakes off our helping hands and sits down on the curb.

I let her rest—I turn to Nadia instead. "Okay," I say. "They're eating people's tides… which means, what, their magic? Milly, that's what you heard them 'say' back there, right? About the tides?"

"Yeah," Milly says. She's no longer rubbing her temples. "They wouldn't shut up about it. Up close it was deafening. Don't ask me *how* in the heck I could understand what they were saying."

"That's why we brought you here," Nadia says. "And you mentioned Bloated Belly, Fifty Furred Limbs."

"*You* recognized the name," I say sharply. "Who or what is that?"

"I don't think we should linger here," Nadia says, looking uncomfortable. "After the grand buffet downtown... they might still be hungry for dessert."

I let out a gust of annoyed breath. "Nadia. Bloated Belly. That's not someone with indigestion, is it?"

She gives me a wry smile. "No. But I'm not sure how much I can talk about it without..." She uses her hand to mime strangling herself. The self-imposed geas. "You already know that the Hand That Never Closes is the master of quintessence Ports, and the Bloody Swarm rules over water Ports. The Avid Worm is the master of fire Ports..."

"Bloated Belly, Fifty Furred Limbs—that's the whole name?—is the master of earth," I say slowly. "Its spiders are burrowing through the fucking ground."

Nadia nods.

Fifty Furred Limbs. "Is it a spider itself? Like, a mother spider?"

"Well..." she says. "Is the Hand That Never Closes really a hand?"

All this talk of the god I'd rather not think about is stirring a whisper in the back of my mind. *Yes and no. Yes and no...*

I grimace and try to concentrate on the conversation. "Okay. Okay. But we went through an *air* Port to get here, did we not?"

"Therein is the problem," Nadia says. "Bloated Belly doesn't *belong* here. Someone must have let it in."

In a flash I understand, on a deeper level, Nadia's words as soon as she saw the ruin of Portsmouth$_2$. *Did I... did we...?*

And then, *the anxiety of influence.* "You're afraid one of your people cross-contaminated this world, somehow," I say.

Nadia's shoulders drop. "Yeah. It could be. I've never seen anything like this happen, but—"

"Hey, hey hey hey," Arreth says, struggling to her feet to confront Nadia. Storm clouds brew on her face and surpass the winces of pain. "*What* did you say? *You* and *your people* caused the spiders?!"

"I mean," Nadia says, raising an eyebrow, "it's a possibility. I'm not saying that it def—"

"Fuck you!" says the woman with your face. She shoves Nadia, even though the motion sends her own body off balance. Arreth teeters. "*How?! WHY?!!*"

I grab Arreth—not to stop her from attacking Nadia, who is in more than enough shape to defend herself, but to keep her from falling on her face. She twists in my grip and bares her teeth at me, and I say in my cop voice, "That's enough!"

"Let go of me, you Bhadun," she hisses at me, "you bitch!"

I don't. "None of us have the whole story right now," I say. "That's what we're trying to get at. So calm the fuck down and we'll all get the answers we need. Okay?"

She stares at me, and I shake her. "*Okay?*" I repeat. "We'll leave you here as spider food if you don't chill out."

I feel ill touching her, threatening her, when she looks so goddamn much like you. When I'm done speaking, I break and look away, letting her go. Fortunately, Arreth has already taken my point. The tension eases in her and she says, "Okay. All right." She still looks miserable, but she takes a seat on the curb again and sighs, clutching her leg as the pain demands her focus.

Nadia's eyes, which had gone almost dark when Arreth

got in her face, now seem to lighten. She takes a couple of deep breaths as if to center herself and then squats by Arreth.

"I lead a group of explorers," she says. "Our homeworld contains many doorways to other worlds, of which this world is one. We explore those worlds in the hope of higher understanding—of the multiverse, of ourselves. But we, erhm, come in peace. We don't come to places like this to conquer them or destroy them."

Her words have a whiff of rehearsal, as if this is all part of the recruitment package for the cult. Arreth gives her an unsmiling look. "You must not be a very good leader, if you don't know what your 'explorers' have been up to."

Nadia nods, slowly and patiently. She is now fully in control of herself. "You're right. Maybe I should have called myself a coordinator, not a leader... I don't seek to dictate other Portwalkers' actions, only to offer them guidance. Once someone has joined our group, they have full access to all the information we currently have on how to open the Ports—doors—and where each Port goes."

"No restrictions," I ask, "not even on the dangerous places? Like, does *everyone* in your group now know how to get to the City of Games?"

"The most dangerous thing in Avariccia was Scott Shaughnessy," Nadia replies. "But I take your point. No, there are no restrictions. We only admit people that we trust into the Portwalkers."

"Like Graham Tsoukalas," I say.

She frowns at that. "Graham was a bad call. I'll give you that. Poor kid. But—listen, everyone *else* in the group understands their responsibilities and the risks of opening a bad Port. They take them seriously."

Right. So our suspect list includes a significant number

of these serious, responsible people. I don't bother asking Nadia how many Portwalkers there are, because I'm sure that's another "classified" piece of information that would set her geas buzzing. I bet there are dozens, at least. Including the three specimens we saw lounging in the Lord house... what was it, Donna and Erica or Erikka? And Chola, the weird-ass drummer for the Hairlesss Werewolves. Oh yeah, *he* sure seemed serious and responsible.

"Well," Arreth grumbles, "it seems like a damn irresponsible way to travel to other universes."

Nadia and I glance at each other. Neither of us makes an effort to mention that you, Arreth's alternate self, were one of the most gung-ho interdimensional adventurers in the group.

"Let's shelve this for now," I say. "We have to get to Boston-two. Somehow." I glance at Arreth and feel my heart sink—injured like that, she's going to slow us down no matter what. "Arreth, do you have a car?"

She lets out a harsh laugh. "Even if I did, have you seen the fucking roads around here? They're bound to be as bad all the way down to the City of Notions. You're gonna need something hardier." She pauses, then amends herself. "We're gonna need."

Off-roading. Fun. And there's that odd nickname for Boston$_2$ again. I glance up at the wreck of the Portsmouth$_2$ PD. Then I'm struck by a sudden idea. If their garage is anywhere near as sturdy as ours was... "Let's get up to the complex and see if anything's, hmm, miraculously intact. Pray to Fath for us, Arreth."

"You better not be mocking me *or* Fath the Giver—you need all the help you can get, and you're in *my* world, Divya. Divya-*one,* I should say." She grunts and then says, "Well, help me up already."

We make our slow way up the hill. During that interminable walk, an important detail of the spider attack flashes back into my mind. Nadia, a native of *my* world, cast a *spell* to create illusory copies of Arreth that allowed the real Arreth to escape. She used magic!

"Hey, Nadia," I say as I help Arreth negotiate the battered slope up to the municipal complex lot. "What you did in the heat of the moment... I wasn't seeing things, was I?"

"No."

"Milly$_2$ called you a mindfucker. Just like the sailor who created the illusion of a spider lurking outside the Eostrix. She said..." What did she say? It's falling into place now. "She said it was like you'd never used your tide before. But this... this was using your tide, wasn't it?"

Nadia sneaks a glance at me, almost shyly. "I thought I ought to give it a try. I had nothing to lose. This world—I think it awakens the magic in us, somehow. Even though we're not from here." She pauses. "You should try to wake yours up."

Creep magic. I'm not sure I want to see what that looks like. I remember Nadia saying, the last time we were here, that "creeps" had the power to infuse life or take it away. Something about that concept makes my brain itch in recognition, trying to place it in a different context, but I can't make the right neurons fire.

"If these spiders feed off magic," I say, "then don't we *not* want to use it at all?! Wouldn't we be making ourselves targets?"

That wipes the sly grin off her face. "Oh. Shit."

"I think I'll refrain from spellcasting," I say.

The municipal lot is strewn with wreckage and the pulped remains of vehicles, like in Market Square$_2$. City

Hall$_2$ is the pulverized ghost structure that my own Portsmouth's libertarians always wanted to see. However, the back half of the police station is comparatively intact. I find an opening into the hazardous-looking jumble of leaning walls and rubble piles.

"I'm going in," I tell the others. "Be right back."

Milly cocks her head and takes a couple of steps forward, feeling out the building space ahead of us. "You sure? You don't have anything to protect your noggin. Want to borrow my helmet?"

I shake my head, not attracted by the thought of constant proximity warnings in my ears. "I'll keep an eye out."

No one volunteers to join me. I go in and wend my way down the broken halls, hit periodically by painful, doubled flashbacks—to times of relative peace, when I walked the halls of my own version of this place, and to the time of Benazir's attack on the station, all blood and thundering shots. I should have checked to see if there was a way around the back of this wrecked place... but no, I needed to access *this* particular door on the inside. I reach a hand for the knob.

It's unlocked. I swing the door open on the PD's special garage space, walled by concrete.

An ATV, undamaged, beckons to me.

9

The garage door's opening mechanism is busted. But with some elbow grease, I manage to haul it up manually. I climb into the ATV and switch it on. It clicks for a second, stopping my heart, and then the engine roars to life.

I steer the ATV over the path of least resistance through the junk of the station. The look on my companions' faces is priceless when they see the ugly vehicle rattling toward them. Milly can't see it, of course, but she's no dummy—she knows the sound. "Is that an ATV?!" she yells over the engine.

I laugh. "You bet your ass it is," I say. "Hop in, everyone."

Nadia gives Milly a hand inside the ATV. Arreth wrinkles her nose, running her fingers through her dense curls and staring at the ATV, then finally sighs and gets in too. Good thing it's a four-seater.

"Remember," Nadia says from the shotgun seat beside me, "we should stay away from crowds. The denser the concentration of magic, the more likely that the spiders will show up again."

"My thoughts exactly," I holler back. "I'll stay off 95 and Route 1." It being summer here too, if Portsmouth$_2$ has anything approaching the level of tourist season that Portsmouth does, the major highways were jammed with cars when the spiders first struck. The magic-eaters would have been drawn to all those people, and might be still. Maybe all the drivers are corpses by now, but we shouldn't investigate the matter more closely.

I gun it down the slope to the street and bang a left, heading up to the hill to South Street$_2$ and weaving around sinkholes and piles of debris. The ATV's top speed is around ten miles an hour, but that's a hell of a lot better than hoofing it, particularly with an injured person in the party. At the corner of South Street Cemetery$_2$, I turn left onto Sagamore Ave$_2$ and take it south; it'll bring us down to a tiny traffic circle where we can hook onto 1A$_2$ south along the tiny New Hampshire$_2$ coast.

There are a ton of beaches along Route 1A$_2$, but I'm banking on not many people remaining out there in the open sunning themselves at this stage of the spider apocalypse. We should be okay until we hit Salisbury Beach$_2$ in Massachusetts$_2$ and 1A$_2$ turns back inland to meet up with Route 1$_2$ running through Newburyport$_2$. Then I'll have to figure out the next step of the plan; tourist-happy Newburyport$_2$ will be as much of a shitstorm as Portsmouth$_2$ was.

I realize belatedly that Arreth should be sitting in shotgun, not Nadia. I keep having to turn around in my seat and confirm directions with her, in case Portsmouth$_2$ geographically deviates from Portsmouth in some significant way. So far, it doesn't. The only differences I've noticed are surface details: crescents and eyes topping the gravestones in South Street Cemetery$_2$ instead of crosses and Stars of David; Jones Avenue is now Lathans Avenue; the Golden Egg breakfast joint on Sagamore Creek is now Owl's Hatchling, etc.

At least with Nadia up front, I can pepper her with questions about why, exactly, these things have changed when little else has.

"Okay," I say to her over the engine noise. "Stop me if I'm wrong. But it seems like the whole Judeo-Christian thing never freaking happened here. This Fath religion came about instead, though it followed a similar path."

"That's—about what I've guessed too," Nadia says. "But who *is* Fath?"

"Fath is the Giver," Arreth shouts at us from the back seat. "He's the one who gifted us all with magic in the first place. Though—there are some minor branches of Fath worship that would disagree."

"Violently disagree?" I ask her.

She scoffs. "They wish."

"What I meant," Nadia says peevishly, "is—is Fath basically a different name for the Christian God? Did the presence of magic in this world cause the change in name? Or does it go deeper than that?"

"I was going to ask *you* those questions," I say. "You're supposed to be the one with a clue, Miss Explorer of Worlds."

Nadia makes a face at me. "Do you know how many worlds I've seen at this point? This is a relatively minor one among many. Why would I spent a ton of time trying to decipher it?"

"Minor? Fuck you!" comes the retort from the back seat. Followed quickly by a cry of pain as we jolt over a rough patch of road.

"Sorry, Arreth," I shout back. Then I blink. "*Arreth.*

Hannah is a biblical name, and the Bible doesn't exist here. That's why you're not named Hannah."

"I'm not named Hannah because... I'm named Arreth," she replies grumpily.

"Let me guess. 'Arreth' is a character from the Book of Fath, or whatever your main religious text is."

"Uh—yeah," she answers, sounding surprised. "She asked Fath to make her fertile. Then when He did, she sang a beautiful song of giving thanks that rang out across the city and inspired everyone who heard it. Her song was one of the Hundred Deeds that grew Fath's magic inside humanity."

"Okay."

A flipped-over car adorns the center of the little traffic circle. The pavement is torn up but we bump our way over it. I steer us toward 1A. Soon the crashing waves of the Atlantic$_2$ come into view over the seawall. The sun has come out from behind a thick cloudbank, beating down on our exposed heads; it's ideal weather for a swim in the frigid water. We see no one on the beaches but plenty of wrecked vehicles and sinkholes along the road. Eventually I spot a couple of ragged, backpack-toting survivors walking along the top of the high border separating 1A from the sea. They stare at us as we drive by.

"Do you have a plan?" Arreth says, breaking the silence. "For getting rid of the spiders?"

Ah yes, Nadia's promise. I glance at her. She says, "We brought along Milly. And now you know that the spiders feed off your tide. You know they're creatures stemming from Bloated Belly, Fifty Furred Limbs. The first step to a plan is gathering all available information."

"A gentle reminder," I put in. "This impossible mission of yours must take a back seat to the mission of getting down to Boston-two as quickly as possible. Ethan can only put off Benazir's dissection for so long without arousing suspicion."

"You *will* do both 'missions,' as you call them," Arreth speaks up. "I said I'd take care of the survivors in Portsmouth. I speak for them."

Her arrogant tone—*your* arrogant tone, it's one and the same—causes me to blow up. "What survivors?!" I snarl. "Did you see the way we left your city? How many people do you think are still alive back in the Eostrix?"

Arreth flattens against the back of her seat. I chew my lip in regret.

We wind around the modest cliffs of Rye_2, the magnificent estates of the wealthy in tatters. No one in the ATV speaks except for Milly, who occasionally mutters to herself something like "Nuts," or "No, not here." I wonder how much she's picking up the spiders' voices. Enough of that inhuman lust for flesh and life essence has got to drive the listener mad.

The seaside scenery blurs as I focus on the road, trying not to jar us too much as we cross over debris piles so that it won't set off the pain in Arreth's leg. Then, abruptly, Nadia sits up straight in her seat and cranes her neck, peering into the distance.

"Sand sculptures," she says. "The Hampton Beach sand sculpture contest—they do it here too. Divya, look!"

Whatever it takes to put my companions in better spirits. I'm not exactly speeding by the beach, so we have plenty of time to take in the elaborate sand sculptures. The first thing I notice is that they're huge: bigger than the annual sculpture efforts that I remember back in my world. The second is that they're untouched by devastation. Every detail remains pristine.

Then I focus on the content of the sculptures themselves. I have to force myself to keep one eye on the road; these pieces of sand art are all depicting unfamiliar scenes. I glance back at Arreth. "Can you interpret?" I ask, gesturing at the sculptures.

"Uh... sure," she says. "Well, that one is Thephal meeting her owl, obviously."

The sculpture shows a woman with long hair blowing behind her (how did they get the sand to stay like that?), reaching out to a large owl with its wings outstretched. The woman's fingertip and the tip of the owl's claw are the only point of contact between the two figures.

"And that one?" Nadia asks.

I draw in a breath as I see the sculpture she's pointing at: it's a stepped landscape with two principal figures. One is the same long-haired woman from the previous sculpture. She's raising her hands in supplication to the other figure, who's turning away from her; it's a man in a long robe with a haughty expression.

"Bhadun betraying Thephal," Arreth says. "In the Hanging Gardens."

She sweeps her arm toward a third sculpture. "And that's Fath the Giver, bestowing His magic on the people."

The five people with their limbs outstretched, they're clear enough, but what the hell is that *thing* floating above them, shining rays into them? It's shaped like a crescent moon but somehow it's not solid—the sculptor managed to give the thing a wispy look, not an easy feat with solid sand. It's studded with eyeballs of all sizes and with different pupils... some human-looking, some with the vertical slash of prey animals' eyes.

Nadia chokes at the sight of it. "Wait a minute," she says. "Wait a damn minute. *That's* Fath?"

"Yeah..." Arreth says, shooting her a curious look. You know Fath after all?"

"Its name isn't Fath," Nadia chokes out. "And it's not a damn *giver*!"

"Then what—" I stop speaking as I notice a mass of people up ahead at the Sea Shell Stage$_2$, an amphitheater on the beach across the street from the strip of arcades and t-shirt shops and ice cream places. The crowd overflows from the benches of the amphitheater onto the road. This area is tourist ground zero for Hampton Beach in my world, but of course all the tourists around here would be either dead or fled. This must be a group of folks banded together for survival, though they sure are making a lot of noise. I can hear it before the others—a rhythmic chanting. Not "*Fath the Giver*," but "*Fath the Protector*." And periodically a male voice exhorting them; it strikes a chord of recognition in my head.

Hmm.

I slow down. Crowds attract spiders. All that juicy magic energy. We don't want to be anywhere near these people. "Idiots," I say. "Religious idiots at that. I'll take a right somewhere and try to find a way through town around them."

"What if there are even more people in the town proper?" Nadia says. "Can you drive over the beach instead?"

The rock barrier between the beach and the road is high here. "I'll have to get closer to find a better onramp onto the beach if I'm gonna do that."

"Don't!" Arreth says sharply.

I brake the ATV but keep the engine running.

"I know this congregation," she goes on. "Anti-magic nutsos. They're gonna—I can't imagine the apocalypse has made them *less* crazy. Turn around and find a wide berth to take around them. Please, Divya."

A few of the people in the crowd have broken off to approach us, maybe out of curiosity. I sit up, surprised by the latest snatch of fanatic doggerel my ears picked up from the preacher somewhere in the crowd. It was something like *"...and soeth He say, 'Wanton use of demonic powers will bring about My wrath and your destruction...'"* But it's not the words themselves that shock me, it's finally recognizing the high and thready voice speaking them.

"I *know* that guy," I exclaim. "The preacher. Theo LaPlante. Same guy who has a funny top hat and a public-access religious show in Portsmouth, in our world. He's harmless."

"*Turn around*," Arreth shrieks and slams her fist into my shoulder. "Father LaPlante is the worst of 'em!"

I throw the gear into reverse, belatedly realizing I've committed the error that Trig warned me about. Again. Thinking I know something or someone over here because I know it back home. The men walking toward us are no longer walking, and I see now that they have rifles.

I get us turned around, but now shots are firing. With the ATV's pathetic top speed, I don't like our odds of escaping without bullets in our backs. Nadia snatches the pistol from my belt and fires at the riflemen, but the shots don't land—they're out of pistol range.

We need cover. I steer for the wreck of a big truck nearby to hide behind. But before I get there, the rifles let out a couple more pops and one of our tires hisses. *Shit!*

The ATV makes it to the truck cover. Before the crowd disappears from my field of view, I see a couple of figures on bicycles coming up behind the riflemen. That's it. We're screwed. I never thought a stupid bicycle would spell my doom.

"We'll have to make a break for it on foot," I say.

"Fath dammit, Divya!" Arreth snarls. "You forget about my fucking leg? And what about Milly here?"

"I'll go down fighting," Milly says quietly. "They'll underestimate me. I can take at least a couple down."

No. No, no, no. "You're not fighting anyone," I say. "*I'll* provide cover so the rest of you can escape. Arreth, put your pain in a little box you can unwrap later and get ready to leg it. Nadia, give me the goddamn gun back."

"No!" she says, looking horrified.

Arreth lets out a loud, disgusted laugh. "All of you fucking martyrs should have thought about not wrecking my world in the first place!"

We never make it out of the ATV before gunmen swarm around the wrecked truck. Nadia lays the Glock down on the dashboard, realizing the hopelessness of our situation, and says, "We surrender. We surrender!"

"Smart," says a ruddy-faced teenager holding a rifle, a Ruger 10/22 by the look of it.

Arreth whispers a curse behind me but makes no move to defy the surrender. Milly mutters, "Another day, another fight."

"We don't wish to fight you," the teenager replies. "As Father LaPlante always says—it's a glorious day for redemption."

10

LaPlante$_2$'s riflemen order us out of the ATV. They all have Ruger 10/22s—must have been a sale at Kittery Trading Post$_2$. They're thrown off by eyeless Milly in her helmet. One of them mutters, "Fath stripped her of sight for her sins," but another disagrees. They conclude the holy father will be able to explain this strange interloper.

As the riflemen lead the four of us toward the crowd, I notice that people are heading out of the amphitheater and toward the beach.

"Service is over," says the armed teenager. He looks oddly familiar. "But Father LaPlante is about to perform another miracle."

"What's your name, kid?" I ask.

"Roderick," he says. Okay, that doesn't ring a bell; must just be the fanaticism, which I saw plenty of not so long ago in the City of Games. His eyes have a shine to them as he speaks—he's a true believer, not hired muscle.

"The miracle will make you *believe*," says another rifleman, a tall man with a virulent case of adult acne.

"Who says we don't?" I say.

"*I* don't," Arreth speaks up angrily.

"Most don't," says Roderick. "That's why Fath the Protector had to plague the world. We needed a new beginning, to honor Fath and cast away our sinful demon worship. That's what Father LaPlante says."

They lead us onto the beach. I see now that there's a tent city, which is where most of the crowd is headed. As we trudge across the sand, Milly grips my arm. "There's one coming," she hisses.

"Spider?" I murmur low enough for our escort not to hear.

She nods and repeats the word more loudly, misjudging her own voice's volume. "Yes! *Spider!*"

The tall man looks over. "How do you know, freak?"

"She doesn't," I say, shoving her hand away. I'm cheered by the possibility of a spider coming to destroy us—because at least it'll take out these fuckers too.

"It's coming," Milly says. "We have to go! All of you do!"

"We're not letting you go, so don't try these dumb tricks," Roderick says. "Stop. Once you see what Father LaPlante is capable of, you won't want to leave anyway."

We come into the midst of the ragged collection of tents, and there he is, old Crazy Theo himself. Except Theo LaPlante$_2$ carries himself with much more dignity and confidence than I've ever seen my world's Theo LaPlante display, and this one is surrounded by beaming followers. He's wearing a black cassock covered with silver crescents and a necklace with beads painted to look like eyes. He also, notably, lacks a top hat.

"What a pleasure it is to meet new friends," Father LaPlante$_2$ says. "We have *so much* to discuss, but you must forgive me... I have a task to perform first. I'd hate to disappoint my flock."

"Divya, goddammit, we need to run," Milly says frantically. "I don't care if they shoot us in the back—better than getting ripped apart by—"

"Stop it," I snap at her. By now I can hear traces of it too, detect the faint vibration. But I think of the spider as an opportunity. Optimistic to the end, I suppose, but what if we can use it somehow to escape like we escaped from the sailors in Portsmouth$_2$?

Then LaPlante$_2$ surprises me by saying, "A spider? No reason to fear—you are under Fath's protection here. Wait where you are." And he strides off toward the edge of camp, exactly in the direction of the vibrations.

"What's he *doing*?" Nadia says.

"Watch," the teenager orders.

I notice that the pavement on the road bordering the beach is ripped up and full of sinkholes. LaPlante$_2$ walks away from the camp on sandaled feet. He stops on the sand, still a good distance away from the road, and that's when a monstrous spider bursts out from the road.

It's as vile-looking as the other ones we've seen, though removed from the immediate threat, I can get a clearer look at it. The tangle of hairy legs includes legs growing out from *other* legs. Fully extracted from the ground, the spider displays a pale, smooth belly—though not particularly bloated. (Maybe only Bloated Belly itself can lay claim to that honor.) Its scimitar-like pincers work fast at the air.

It takes a step in Father LaPlante$_2$'s direction.

"*CREATURE OF FATH!*" he bellows at the spider, standing his ground. "*YOU HAVE COME TO A GATHERING OF THE GOD'S FAITHFUL CHILDREN!*"

The spider skitters closer. It screeches.

Milly moans, "It wants all of us. The things it's saying..."

"*WE HAVE SURVIVED FATH'S JUDGMENT!*" LaPlante$_2$ shouts. "*WE HAVE OBSERVED THE LORD'S LESSON! WE DO NOT PRACTICE MAGICS HERE. BEGONE!*"

The spider's legs touch down on the sand. Then it stops.

"*BEGONE!*" the preacher shouts. "*GO AND SEEK OUT THE UNFAITHFUL AND DEVOUR THEM! BEGONE FROM HERE!*"

The spider remains still for several seconds. Then it skitters back away and climbs into one of the sinkholes in the road, disappearing from view.

Father LaPlante$_2$ turns back to the tent city and raises both arms. His congregation erupts into applause and cheering and screaming. "*Praise Father LaPlante! Praise Fath the Protector!*"

He walks back toward us and Milly mutters, "Jesus Christ. It's gone."

"Jesus isn't here right now," Nadia says grimly.

Three dozen of LaPlante$_2$'s faithful mob him, touching the hems of his cassock and falling down at his feet. But the preacher manages to navigate his way around them with a hurried blessing here and there, and he comes back to where we're being held.

He snaps his fingers and several women nearby scramble to attention. LaPlante$_2$ nods his head at them. "Would you fetch us some seats and some iced tea? I have a few matters to discuss with our prospective congregants."

∼

TEENAGE RODERICK and the other riflemen remain nearby

with watchful gazes, but my companions and I are permitted to take a seat in frayed camp chairs arranged in a small circle. LaPlante$_2$ sits lightly and regards us before speaking. The women silently bring us warm cans of "iced" tea and confiscate our bags.

"You witnessed the miracle," the preacher says, regarding us with an expressionless face. I can tell he'll be less funny than the LaPlante I know from local TV.

"That was no miracle," Arreth says. "Fath has no use for frauds like you."

As always, our truculent friend is showing little interest in negotiation (or bucket-filling). But LaPlante$_2$ regards her calmly and says, "Fath the Protector worked through me to shield the congregation from his own instruments of retribution."

"So you said," I put in. "You called the spider a 'creature of Fath.'"

Father LaPlante$_2$ nods. "The spiders have come from Fath Himself to cleanse the world of sin. Like Fath scoured the earth clean with windstorms long ago, in the days before the Hundred Deeds. The time has come once again for people to remember that magic is demonborn and sinful."

"Magic comes from *Fath*," Arreth growls.

"So goes the heresy," Father LaPlante$_2$ says. "Fath is not the source of magic, nor has He ever been."

"Actually, I think he's right, about that at least," Nadia speaks up.

I can't believe she's agreeing with the preacher. And neither can Arreth, who throws her a death glare.

"Fath is a big fat fraud," Nadia goes on, and now, of course, she's lost them both. I, however, sit forward in my chair. "What you think of as 'Fath' is in reality a g—"

Her eyes bulge. She gasps and pinches her neck with her fingers. The damn geas is kicking in. This happened to Sol a couple of times when he was trying to explain the beings behind the Ports; it was scary then and this is scary now. "Stop," I say.

I move toward her, but a rifleman barks at me, "*Sit down!*"

I plant my ass back in the chair. "It's okay," I say softly to Nadia. "It's okay, I get it." And I think I *am* getting it, weirdly enough.

She presses her lips together, as if signaling to her Compass that she's gotten the message. Gradually she relaxes. Her fingers drop from her neck and her generous lips open, exhaling grateful breath.

"You sick or something?" LaPlante$_2$ asks her.

"She's fine," I say. Then I add, louder, "We're *all* going to be quiet now and give you a chance to, um, further elaborate on your religion." I hope the others will get it. The more we know, the more chance of finding a loophole to exploit.

LaPlante$_2$'s mouth twists. "This isn't about me talking. This is about you finding your salvation. I am here to give you a chance to get right with Fath, do you understand? I don't know how you've survived the apocalypse so far, but submitting to Fath the Protector is the only way you'll make it any further."

Because the good father will kill us if we don't.

"The world fell too much in love with itself and shunned the face of Fath," the preacher goes on. "Not just through practicing *magic,* but sinking so much time into fey pursuits. Liberal arts, liberal tolerances, all the Notions that spread from Boston through the generations to infect the rest of New England. Do you even remember this country was founded by good folk who shunned magic in all its forms? They used to *burn* practitioners, and while I cannot advocate that level of violence... well, children, I say they had the right idea."

There it is again—*Notions*. I can hear the capital N in his voice, like when Milly$_2$ and Arreth said it. I still harbor a faint hope that we'll actually make it to Boston$_2$, so I press for details. "Do you think Boston—" I stop myself from saying *Boston-two*— "has been hit hard by the spiders, then? If they're instruments of Fath's will?"

Father LaPlante$_2$ looks at me sharply. "Yes, you *would* want to know that, wouldn't you? Where else would a carful of godless women heading south be going?"

Hm. I've accidentally stepped in it. But I'm not sure yet what "it" is. "I have relatives there," I lie. "I haven't heard from them."

"You have arrived at your destination already," LaPlante$_2$ says. "This will be your home now. The City of Notions is a smoking ruin thanks to the judgment of Fath—count yourself lucky that you encountered my flock along the way."

His words sicken my hopes, though I insist to myself, *He's lying*. I manage to say, "Thanks, but I'd rather check it out down there for myself."

"No," says Father LaPlante$_2$. "All of you *will* stay here and embrace Fath and family." He glances at Milly and frowns. "Even the one in the helmet, whose wickedness hath caused her very eyes to flee from her head. You will all relearn your place. The Notion of feminism is one of the diseases that must be stamped out if we are to shape a new world that pleases Fath the Protector. You will be wives and mothers to my faithful men."

"That's not for us," I say before the others can word their objections more strongly.

"Ah." LaPlante$_2$ gives me an unbalanced grin and shows me too much of his corneas. His white hair may be combed here and he may have brainwashed a hundred people, but he's the same crazy bastard he is back in my world. If I ever get home, I'm going to petition to get LaPlante off the air. "Who would so roundly reject the grace of the Protector but those in the grip of demon worship?"

His followers nearby murmur their agreement. Well, his male followers; the women, as usual, have nothing to say. I can't hold back a shiver. What has he done to them? Or what have they done to themselves?

My anger is cold and massive, an iceberg ready to lance through to the surface. The old Divya would have let it out by now. But I've appointed myself a speaker for Nadia and Arreth and Milly; all of our lives are at stake.

"We're not into demons," I say. "We don't practice magic, either. We—ehrm—thank you very much for your kind invitation into your church, but you won't find us to be enthusiastic followers. Or wives. Our cooking sucks and we're totally bad in bed, so why don't you let—"

"*Liar*," says LaPlante$_2$ dramatically and rises from his camp chair. He points at Nadia. "That one has the *stink* of magic on her. Used not so long ago. You are a muddler of men's minds."

Nadia sighs and throws up her hands. "Whatever."

"And the mutant," LaPlante$_2$ says, gesturing at Milly, "she dares to listen in on the speech of Fath's holy instruments. That is blasphemy."

"Yeah, she predicted the spider coming," says the teenager with the rifle.

LaPlante$_2$ indicates Arreth next. "The dark one, she accesses forbidden knowledge of a different sort. Reaching into the past, where none but Fath should see."

"Call me Arreth," Arreth says, "and I won't call you the shriveled old one."

Somehow the preacher can sense magic and its types, like Milly (and the late Milly$_2$) can. My thoughts are whirring. I wonder if, like Milly, he too can hear the voices of the spiders and thus predict their arrival. That might help him stage his "miracles" on the regular... but why *had* the spider stopped and retreated?

He turns back to me. "You..." he says, "it's faint but it's there. You could meddle in the cycle of life and death. But I can't tell if you ever have used that magic. You may be the one in your little band of sinners with the greatest hope of redemption."

By now I've realized, though, that Father Theo LaPlante$_2$ never had any intention of "redeeming" us. He knew all along that most of us used magic. This whole conversation has been a farce acted out for his followers, to show the wickedness of us four "godless women" and justify whatever he's planning to do next.

"Not interested," I say.

Father LaPlante$_2$ shakes his neatly combed head in mock sadness. "I don't give up on sinners that easily. Even Thephal could be persuaded to give up her vile magical arts when the right man with a strong hand entered her life."

"That's *not* what happened," Arreth says fiercely.

He ignores her and addresses his flock. "Tonight, then, we will have a ceremony of exorcism at the New Church of Fath. We will drive the demons and the magic out of these wayward children. Go and gather the faithful, my friends! Seek them in Hampton and beyond and return with them at sundown to the New Church. We will fill the pews and we will show the Protector our devotion! Go!"

Our guards remain, but a sizable portion of the tent city

inhabitants heed Father LaPlante$_2$'s call and head for the road beyond the beach. I watch them go, noting how they scatter, traveling in only twos and threes and leaving a wide distance between each grouplet.

"You trained them to do that," I say to him. "Didn't you? You know the spiders are more likely to attack big crowds. But how do you keep the spiders away from this tent city—and from your church services?"

"You will come to believe in miracles too, child, in time," he says. Then he walks away and leaves us with our captors.

The day proceeds in agonizing slowness. We bake in the sun, the tents so close and yet so far. I squirm in my camp chair, driven slowly madder by the thought that every hour wasted here is another hour Jeong will need to forestall Benazir's execution. Another hour closer to failure. Nadia scoots her chair closer to mine, sensing my agitation, and leans her blonde head on my shoulder until one of LaPlante$_2$'s men orders her away. Arreth seems disturbed by the time passing too, bobbing her knee incessantly (as you often did), probably thinking about all the lives in Portsmouth$_2$ snuffing out as the hours drag on.

Meanwhile, Milly Fragonard leans against her chair and tilts her head back, listening to the secret music of the spiders' hungry cries. Occasionally she mutters "Give it up," or asks "Where is *it*, exactly?" as if they can hear her respond. She removes her helmet and places it in her lap, shaking out her sweaty dark hair and rubbing at the corners of eyes that are not there.

Any time the four of us exchange more than a few words with each other, one of the guards steps in and tells us to clam up. They all keep using that phrase—*clam up*—and then grin at each other when they think we're not looking. Yes, guys, I get it, we're on a goddamn beach. At least

LaPlante$_2$ hasn't wrung the sense of humor out of them. Although none of the women are laughing.

They do keep us hydrated. Wouldn't want any of us to pass out during the big show tonight. As Roderick the ruddy-faced teenager brings me another bottle of water, I ask him, "Where is this New Church?"

He laughs. "You're lookin' at it." He points across the street from the Sea Shell Stage$_2$ at a long, low building, lined with windows, topped by a blue roof: the Casino Ballroom$_2$. Back home, the Ballroom is a Hampton Beach institution that draws both up-and-coming performers and has-been acts staging a comeback. Here, it's seen better days. I see a poster hanging near the Casino Ballroom$_2$'s vertical sign and digital marquee. The poster proclaims:

The International Sensation is Coming Home!
HAIRLESS WEREWOLVES
Back to the Seacoast for One Night Only!

The poster bemuses me. I guess the Hairless Werewolves$_2$ made it a lot bigger than their counterpart in my world. Then I notice that two messages are flashing in rotation on the marquee itself:

FATH SAVES
MAGIC DAMNS
REPENT OR BE
SPIDER FOOD

"You're using the Casino Ballroom for a church?!" I say, snorting.

"Something funny about that?" Roderick says.

I swat a mosquito on my neck. "Not at all. Can I ask what happened to your 'Old Church'?"

"Spiders leveled it. Father LaPlante$_2$ says it was because there were 'too many unbelievers in our midst.' But Fath led him to the Ballroom to reach a bigger audience and save more souls."

Of course. The good father has an explanation for everything. "Kid," I say in a low voice. "Do you believe all this stuff? Or did he force you to convert to his church? Perhaps at gunpoint?"

The teenager responds in a normal volume. "Father LaPlante$_2$ saved my life. He saves all our lives, every day."

"By the way, what all is involved in an exor—"

"That's enough," he says. "Be quiet."

The sun makes its way down toward the town. Knots of people appear in the streets and cross to the tent city, resulting in a population much larger than we saw when we first got here. I wonder if we're the lucky beneficiaries of the first "exorcism" or if they've done this before. Judging by the eagerness and knowing smiles from the crowd hovering nearby, I'm guessing exorcisms have become a regular source of entertainment.

Our captors feed us a humble dinner of snacks and sodas scavenged from some wrecked store. The brand names are unfamiliar but the tastes are more or less the same: high-calorie junk. As the light fades from the sky, Father LaPlante$_2$ gets atop his pulpit in the center of the tent city.

"Come, my people!" he shouts. "To the New Church of Fath, where we will see demons defeated and souls saved!"

The crowd answers with ringing cries of "*Praise Fath!*" and "*Back to Hell with the demons!*" We're forced to our feet. Then the mass of people surges forward, and we're carried along with them at gunpoint, across the beach and Route 1A$_2$ and the board-less "boardwalk," to the Casino Ballroom$_2$. An advance team has prepared the New Church for tonight's business; the lights of the Ballroom$_2$ are ablaze and canned rock music floats out from the venue. Yes, the locals are hyped up and Fath the Protector smiles down on the show tonight...

Do you remember seeing that alt band from the nineties at the Ballroom a couple summers ago? You were drunk before the show even started, and I guess I don't blame you. You'd only been in junior high when this particular band was big. And you were making fun of me the whole week leading up to the show. My musical tastes didn't measure up to your preferences for indie folk and New Age mandolin duos.

But goddamn, did you dance your heart out the entire time. And when the show was over, the moon was so gigantic over our heads as we walked on the beach, like a planet about to collide with Earth.

Tonight, here in nightmare land, the moon is small and partially occluded by clouds as it sharpens in the sky. Not impressive enough, if this is the last moon I'll ever see.

I notice several big holes punched in the slatted boards along the bottom of the building, with only darkness visible within. A basement level. A normal person wouldn't hear the noise coming from the basement, but I haven't been normal for quite some time. Water is sloshing underneath the Ballroom$_2$. Hm.

The performance space is on the second floor, accessible by a narrow outer staircase. On the first floor I see a panoply of arcade and carnival games: skee-ball, balloon busting, basketball throwing, skill cranes, and so forth. Signs are plastered everywhere that say *KNOW-IT-ALLS BANNED FROM PREMISES*. Other signs advertise mini golf and kiddie rides elsewhere in the building.

Nadia takes my hand as we climb the stairs to the Casino

Ballroom$_2$ in the midst of the throng. For once, the guards leave us alone. "I'm sorry," she murmurs.

"This isn't your fault."

"If it was one of my people, then it *definitely* is," she says, shaking her head. "I don't see any other possibility for how this world could turn so quickly—could fall so quickly..."

"Cross-contamination," I say. "Someone let Bloated Belly, Fifty Furred Limbs in."

"It doesn't belong here," she says. "This is an air-aligned world. Though I know now that I didn't fully understand this world even before the spiders showed up to ruin it..."

Her geas kicked in, I remember, right when she was trying to tell us—tell me—how Fath was a "fraud." Her Compass would only intervene if she were about to spill information on Ports, or the masters of Ports. I.e., the stuff that could compromise the Portwalkers and make them vulnerable to outsiders like the city councilors. So, if Fath isn't really Fath, then...

"We got here through an air-affiliated Port. Is 'Fath' a name the master of the air Ports is wearing here?"

Nadia nods vigorously. "That sculpture. That was... you know. I should have realized from all the eye and crescent iconography that's so important to Fath worship."

I still don't know the true name of the air master—or at least, what Nadia knows it by—but I've learned something important. I think. "So this was the air master's turf. And Bloated Belly, the earth master, gains an upper hand, or leg, by getting in here and fucking things up... is that right?"

She loses her grip and gets shoved away from me before she can answer.

The Casino Ballroom$_2$ can seat thousands of people. LaPlante$_2$ won't fill all those seats tonight by any means—but hundreds is an impressive showing, given that this world is under attack. For whatever reason, the venue hasn't suffered any breaches yet from spiders. Maybe it was an off-night when the initial feeding frenzy hit Hampton Beach$_2$. Most of the stage lights are working; as we're hustled up the center aisle through the noisy crowd, I squint at the stage ahead and discern several dark stains on the surface. A few wooden chairs sit on the stage, and a rope pulley dangles from the overhead lights. A rock recording blares from the speakers.

Father LaPlante$_2$, the man of the hour, is not yet onstage. He'll make his theatrical entrance after the four of us have already been deposited there to await our glorious rebirth in Fath's grace. I still don't have a plan. Most of what our little group of godless women has at our disposal really is "dollar magic," worthless when the price of our escape is valued so much higher.

How will LaPlante$_2$ keep spiders away from this ceremony, with all this tantalizing energy gathered in one spot? I spot Milly not far away. She doesn't seem agitated, so there aren't any spiders on the way yet. Or maybe she's given up.

"Let's go," says Roderick. I let him prod me up onto the stage, and the others follow. The armed guards sit us down in the chairs, where we blink under the harsh lights. A cheer erupts from the crowd even though the show hasn't officially started.

I look at the rope pulley and suddenly understand that it's not there to operate a curtain or adjust a stage light.

An unseen audio board operator kills the recorded music. Instantly everyone in the audience falls quiet. Arreth stands up in the silence and screams at them.

"*Thephal's owl eat your eyes, you cowardly fucks!!*"

The teenager shoves her back down. Boos and jeers erupt from the crowd as Father LaPlante$_2$ strides onto the stage from the rear, a mic pinned to the collar of his cassock. He stops and frowns.

I touch Arreth's shoulder. Good on her for spoiling the preacher's entrance, even if we accomplish nothing else before we die.

11

LaPlante₂ lifts his arms and now the applause hits, now the cheering strikes all of us onstage almost violently. I flinch away, press myself against the hard wood of my chair. There's not just rapture but blood in that sound.

"My brothers and sisters in Fath!" he roars when the noise dies down, and that sets it off again. Only after another couple minutes pass can LaPlante₂ begin his sermon.

"We are gathered here through the blessing of the Protector," LaPlante₂ says, his voice thundering through the speakers, "who loves us and shields us from his terrible wrath. Everyone here tonight understands what it means to walk in Fath's footsteps and cast aside the evils of magic use and demon worship.

"Everyone, that is, except for these four women present onstage with me tonight."

We receive a hearty booing. But LaPlante₂ holds up a stiff hand, palm out, and the jeering cuts off.

"I had a vision," he says. "I had a vision, and in Fath's

name it was like nothing I had ever seen. I was standing on the sand of the sacred beach, and I saw a woman ride a spider past me. She was beautiful as the spider was hideous, her hair flowing behind her, and her belly was ripe with child. She rode this monstrous beast like a horse, and she never looked my way, but I *knew* her, and she knew me."

The crowd mutters. Nadia frowns at me and rolls her eyes. Apparently LaPlante$_2$ is going to milk this ceremony for all it's worth.

"That woman," the preacher goes on, "was Thephal, daughter of Fath. The link to Fath was clear, as the spiders are instruments of his vengeance against the unfaithful. And her swollen belly spoke unto me as a symbol of the temptress finally being brought to heel. To renounce her wicked magics and take a man as husband and bear children, as women should. I believed then that we would see the birth of a new world amid all this devastation, a world returning to the fundamentals that Fath loves so dearly.

"And then fate brought these unrepentant women to my very doorstep! Do not jeer them, for they will be the first wicked wantons to be converted to Fath... that is, with your help. Do you wish to help me bring them into the light of Fath?!"

The crowd roars. Yes, yes, naturally they would love to.

"Excellent!" the preacher roars. "Then, shall we *begin*?"

He grabs Nadia by her short hair, hauling her to her feet. She strikes him in the chest with one fist. LaPlante$_2$ takes a step back, wincing, and the tall, acne-pitted man clubs Nadia in the head. She reels.

"The demons are strong in this one!" LaPlante$_2$ says, chuckling.

"Hey. Hey! Stop it!" I holler, kicking my chair over. Before the guards can stop me, I rush to take Nadia's arm.

She leans toward me, but LaPlante₂ has a firm grip on her. Someone grabs me from behind.

"Start with me first," I shout at the preacher. "You can go through all of us, but start with *me*."

He gives me a thoughtful look. "Why?"

"You said, said I had the greatest chance of redemption. Why don't you score an easy win before you move on to... bigger challenges."

"No," Nadia mumbles, but she's clutching her head—the gun butt will have given her a nasty headache.

LaPlante₂ lets Nadia go. Teenage Roderick, the one who grabbed me, thrusts me forward. LaPlante₂ covers his mic with his hand as he murmurs to me, "Do you promise me to *scream*?"

I don't respond. I can't—I'm in the middle of a panic attack. Oh, I'll deliver for the good father, all right. The guard directs me toward one end of the rope pulley.

"What is your name, child?" the preacher asks.

"Divya Allard," I say.

"Take your clothes off, Divya," LaPlante₂ says.

I blink. Oh. There's a humiliation aspect to this, not just pain. Unfortunately for LaPlante₂, I've already been humiliated far more than *this,* with my name dragged through the mud of Portsmouth not once but twice. I've been called a terrorist, a murderer, a traitor to the uniform. I've been cuffed by my former colleagues and held at gunpoint. I've had my *mind* violated by Scott Shaughnessy's terrible tidal rod and been forced to turn on friends, forced to take an innocent life.

This, exposing my diminutive brown body to a bunch of fanatical idiots, this is nothing. I bend and slowly remove my shoes and long white socks. I take off my sailor's shirt and bra and shrug out of my shorts and underwear. I don't turn from the audience but instead face them full on, staring them down and making them complicit.

Roderick, audibly gasping for air, binds my wrists behind my back. Whether out of some last shred of decency or fear of LaPlante$_2$, he doesn't touch me otherwise.

"Our cousins the Europeans, before succumbing to permissive Notions and losing their spines, used to be incredibly skilled at forcing the magic out of people," LaPlante$_2$ says to the audience. "During the Great Questioning, interrogators would use a device called a *strappado* to set the demons inside a person aflame with agony. It is simple, yet reliable and effective. Roderick?"

The ruddy-faced teenager pulls on the other, weighted end of the rope. As the slack cuts out, the rope end tied to my wrists jerks them upward, behind my back. I cry out. The rough material of the rope bites into my flesh. Within a normal range of motion, I can't get my arms much higher than my shoulder blades. But now they bend sharply upward under the force from the rope. I scream.

"Bless this child," LaPlante$_2$ intones, "Fath the Protector. Drive the evil from her and let her walk in Your sacred path. Let her desire to cast spells turn to ash!"

I can't turn around, but I imagine Roderick has help pulling on the rope now. The force seems to double, enough to cause my bare feet to leave the stage. A callous giant is ripping my body apart, limb by limb. I shriek. I can't believe LaPlante$_2$ thought I would have any other option.

"*Let her down!*" someone yells behind me. Milly. I hear a heavy thud, some cruel object striking flesh.

"Do you feel the demons being driven out of you?!" LaPlante$_2$ shouts, though he's not really talking to me. He keeps mugging for the audience. "Is it not the evil in you screaming as it's being forced from your body? *Are the demons fleeing from you?*"

"Yep, all gone," I groan. Another sharp yank and I'm about four feet off the stage. I feel a distinct, excruciating *pop* in both my shoulders. "*AUGH!*"

"Do you feel the light of Fath entering you, Divya Allard?"

Pain is obliterating all my thoughts. It's impossible for me to answer him. The only coherent thought that surfaces is: *I'm flying!* Agony wraps and warps my whole body as its weight pulls down on my fucked arms, gravity having its due.

As I'm about to pass out from the pain, an inhuman voice speaks in the back of my mind. *Divya.*

I'm dangling from my deadening limbs, I'm seeing constellations of pain-stars exploding in front of my eyes, but I recognize the voice—I'll never forget the sound of the monster. The Hand That Never Closes. My eyelids flutter shut and I can almost discern the outline of the huge, corpse-like hand—and the sucking void in the middle of its palm—behind the stars dancing and dying across my vision.

You want a piece of this world too? I ask the Hand in my mind. *Bloated Belly and Fath the Fraud are having it out, but you could make it a three-way fight...*

I have no interest in this ruin, the Hand answers(? *Is* it answering me?). *My interest lies only in you. You are supposed to carry out my will, but you are failing me.*

"Renounce your magic!" the preacher shouts somewhere far away. "Divya Allard, you must renounce it all!"

Then help me, you useless zombie, I mentally beseech the master of quintessence.

What will you sacrifice?

I have nothing left.

You have everything left. For now.

I crack an eye open. At least from my pain-fogged perspective, I seem to be much higher off the ground than before, a broken angel swinging from the festively illuminated rafters. *Happy Strappado, everyone, and to all a good night!*

I'm not sure I'm even capable of speech anymore, but I open my mouth to see if anything comes out.

"Hey, Father!" I shout down. "For a guy so opposed to magic, you sure love using it yourself!"

The crowd grumbles. Father LaPlante$_2$ cranes his neck up at me. I go on, "You could tell what kind of magic I had. And what my friends have! That *sensing* is magic in itself, isn't it?"

"I do not use magic," LaPlante$_2$ says, the speakers shooting his indignant voice throughout the auditorium.

"That's bull," I hear Milly shout. "I have that sense too. I can sense *you*—you're like me, Theo LaPlante. A, a wizard!"

Now the muttering from the crowd grows angrier, and louder. They won't be on our side, but they don't have to be. They just have to turn on LaPlante$_2$.

What will you sacrifice?

Take my goddamn super-hearing. Take my whole ears if you want.

I have no interest in that. Only in life turned to death, and death turned to life.

I jerk downward a few feet and then stop, still in mid-air, the abrupt halt sending a fresh wave of agony through me. One of the rope pullers must be getting tired. I can sense the Hand probing at my mind. I should never have let it inside my cranium in the first place, but then, like now, it had been a desperate situation. The Hand sure loves its sacrifices—they're needed for opening any of its quintessence Ports. But

I'm not about to sacrifice anyone's life to save the sorry one belonging to me.

Choose. One of your friends.

No!

Choose or I will choose.

"Fuck you!" I seethe aloud, wriggling on my line.

I've lost track of what's happening below my *strappado* act. I look down at Father LaPlante$_2$ marching angrily toward my companions, maybe to shut Milly up—she must have hit a nerve. I wonder, again, whether LaPlante$_2$ can sense the spiders coming like Milly can. It would help his "miracles" if he could predict when the spiders arrive. Though I still don't know how he repels them. Unless he does have this fucker Fath on his side, and Arreth has been wrong all this time...

The rope lowers a couple more feet, more gently this time. Maybe the rope handlers don't know what to do while Father LaPlante$_2$ is caught up in his argument with Milly, which I don't have the luxury of following. Then an image of the sand sculptures randomly punches through my brain.

No, not randomly. *Think.* The sculptures were pristine. Unmolested by the spiders, like the tent city itself. Both on the beach.

What if the spiders have an aversion to water—or at least salt water?

That wouldn't explain why they're staying away from the Casino Ballroom$_2$, and have never attacked it—oh. I *heard* the seawater flooding the basement.

"Milly's right, Father," I say with more volume and force than I thought possible, though I won't carry anywhere as far as the miked LaPlante$_2$ himself. Still, as I twist on my rope, I see I've gotten his attention. "You're a liar. And, you know what, you're a fake too."

"Shut your dirty mouth, demons," Roderick says at the other end of my rope. Looks like he's been working it solo after all; he must have a lot more strength than I realized. He jerks on the makeshift *strappado* and I raise a foot back into the air.

I bite back a scream. "Hey! At least let me say why!"

"So? Why?" the teenager asks.

"That's enough," LaPlante$_2$ booms.

I grit the words out. "Have Father LaPlante$_2$ show you a real miracle—have him repel a spider when he's not standing right next to the ocean. Or over it, like we are here. *They fear the water, not him!*"

"Lies! Demons lie!" says LaPlante$_2$ fiercely.

The *strappado* lowers me back down to the floor. It's not much of a relief—my body is still pulling on my damaged arms as I sag in my binds—but I snarl, "Have him prove it!"

"Hoist her back up," LaPlante$_2$ commands Roderick. "The pain is not sufficient yet to exorcise her!"

Instead, the kid lets the rope go altogether. I fall to the stage in a heap. Roderick steps closer to Father LaPlante$_2$, close enough for the preacher's mic to pick him up too. Damn, the kid looks familiar right now. "Can you show us that she lies about the water? Can you drive a spider away farther inland?"

The congregants weren't able to hear my accusations as I made them. But now, via Roderick, they're hearing them secondhand, and it's causing commotion out there in the seats. LaPlante$_2$ looks at his acolyte with plain hatred.

"I don't have to prove anything to you!" he says. "Fath asks for your belief, not your nagging questions!"

Roderick nods. But he's not satisfied, and from what I can hear, a number of folks in the audience aren't either.

One of the other riflemen comes forward and says, "Father, it wouldn't hurt, would it? To quell the doubters?"

"*I will not!*" Father LaPlante$_2$ snaps.

Then a ghost spider appears onstage with us.

It's only there for a second, and it's not even convincing while it is there. The details are rough and the image flickers like a malfunctioning TV. I understand through my pain that Nadia is trying out her magic again, and having a lot worse luck with it than the last time.

However, it's enough to, for that brief second, freak LaPlante$_2$ out and knock him backward on his ass.

The spider sputters out. LaPlante$_2$'s fear and indignity make the audience laugh, drowning out the scattered initial screams. The fanatics present at the Ballroom$_2$ can't resist a good old-fashioned pratfall, and the preacher doing it—well, that takes the cake. Doubting Roderick doubles over with laughter.

"Hey, kid," I hiss at him. "*Please.*"

Roderick looks up. His chuckles fade, but his sides are shaking and tears are streaming from his eyes. He unties my wrists. I'm a crumpled ball of white-hot flames and I don't have the strength to get up. But being free, I dimly register, is a good thing. Roderick meets my eyes briefly, I see Nadia right behind him, and abruptly the family resemblance hits me. The reason that he looked so familiar.

I would bet dollars to fried doughnuts that Roderick's last name is *Lord*. He's the only child of Jim and Phyllis Lord in this world, Nadia's brother from another universe.

LaPlante$_2$ picks himself up from the stage, scowling out at the audience—the laughter hasn't died out yet. He points at the poor teenager. "Did I *tell you to untie her?!*"

I feel hands on me—gentle but insistent hands. Nadia's

saying somewhere above me, "Divya. Talk to me, girl. Are you—"

I lose the rest of what she's saying as the hands (her hands?) pull me up by my shoulders. I scream. And then I feel the vibration of the stage underneath me. This time I don't need Milly to tell me the spiders are coming.

The walls of the Ballroom$_2$ explode inward from all directions, or at least it seems to my confused senses. Voices rise in fear, but it isn't a wordless sound—it has direction. A target. Hundreds of the fanatics are screaming: "*Father LaPlante! Save us, Father! Father, save us!!*" Maybe some are pleading to Fath "Himself" too, but they're drowned out by the appeals to a savior standing right onstage with us.

Except, well, the chitters and screeching of the invading spiders join the din, and the pleas dissolve into animal cries of agony and sheer terror. Father LaPlante$_2$ apparently has not come through for his flock.

More hands on me. Another attempt to lift me, and I shriek again to match my battered body's protest, but this time they keep me upright, and we're moving, as far as I can tell toward the darkness of the backstage.

What follows becomes patchy, as the jostling of our escape intensifies my pain so badly that I keep blacking out. I see scattered images: a hallway; a broken street in the nighttime; an overturned car; a stretch of sand and dried-out seaweed; Arreth falling and Nadia helping her back up; the side of a boat. And through it all, the back of Milly's helmet.

I feel wood beneath me and can assemble more than snatches of my surroundings. I try to raise my head. I'm on a dock; Milly has put me down, and the agony has receded. She and Nadia and Arreth are working on untying a boat from its posts. I roll my head back and see, upside down, a robed figure walking toward them, the moonlight shining off the weapon in his hand.

"Gun! Gun!" I scream. It's all I can manage, but it's enough to get their attention. Arreth turns as the figure fires. Darkness flies from her, as if she's losing her shadow from the inside, and Arreth falls. Milly instinctively crouches at the sound of the gunshot, but Nadia moves toward the assailant. Fearless.

A fresh wave of pain hits me and I fall back. Milly runs toward me, her bat pinnae twitching, and as she scoops me up I black out for good.

Well... not for good, I guess. I do wake up again, but some time has passed, and my location has changed. I'm lying swaddled in a blanket at the bottom of a moving vehicle, moving and rocking—a boat. Speedboat. I'm not the only one lying there, either; Arreth is stretching out beside me, face grey, clutching her bloodied stomach and gasping. Nadia is piloting the boat and screaming something lost in the wind. But Milly is sitting near me. From her outstretched hand, I guess she's the one who shook me awake.

"I'm sorry, Allard," she says. "Nadia says you need to try. She thinks you can help. Arreth is dying."

12

I sit up, trying to suppress my screams at the pain. Arreth does, indeed, look like she's dying, and she's the only one with any advanced medical knowledge. We have no supplies except for the first aid kit lying open near her. Her blood is soaking through the bandages. I blink.

"Wait," I croak. "What am *I* supposed to do?"

"Your magic," Milly says, glancing back at Nadia. "She said you might be able to heal Arreth. If you, like, concentrate enough. Like Nadia did with her illusions."

I make a harsh sound between a laugh and a sob. "I... I can't! Milly, I *can't even move my arms!*"

Milly's mouth twists. I see her sweating. "I'll, I'll put your hands on Arreth for you. Maybe it's like a healing touch thing. That *is* supposed to be your magic here, right?"

"Or—or, wait, it might be a *hurting* magic," I say, remembering. "Nadia, or someone, said 'creeps' could go either way."

But Milly is already moving my hands as delicately as possible to rest atop the mess that is Arreth's stomach. My arms screech at the movement but I bite down on the pain. She moves Arreth's hand out of the way; Arreth is too weak to stop her.

"Nah-ahdia," I groan, trying to make my voice louder and failing. She doesn't turn around. "Damn. Ask her how she made her illusions. What did she do?"

Milly relays my question. Nadia shouts back, "Concentrate! Picture what you want to happen, happening!"

I can barely picture anything right now except for the pain, which pulses through me, in front of me, drawing lightning bolts across my vision. But I squint and take a deep breath and try to channel—*something*—into my hands.

I have no power. I have no magic. This won't work.

Stop it! Try! That's your voice, insistent now.

And indeed, it's coming out of Arreth's mouth—it's the same voice. I don't know if I've been speaking my thoughts out loud. When I look at her, I see you, and that twists me up even more than I'm already twisted. I close my eyes, feeling tears well behind my lids and leak out. *Try. Try. Try.*

Is something sparking from my palms? I don't dare to look. I just try, with all the pitiful remains of my might, to place my hope in my own body and my own self, that I'm transmitting *HEALING* to you, because damn *all* the insane gods, I can't lose you again.

I push forward, eyes shut, willing my broken limbs to come to life and do magic. If I'm a "creep," then so be it. Let me be a creep! Fath the Giver, fucking give me something!

My body spasms—not from pain this time—and I gasp, my eyelids flying open. A feeble light is emanating from my dark, blood-soaked hands. And you're staring at me.

No. Staring through me. Unmoving, robbed of breath. You're dead.

I brush your hands with my fingers; it's about all the

movement I can manage. Nothing. I kiss your lips and they're cold.

"*Hannah,*" I whisper. "No. *Please.* Give me a little more time..."

Milly touches my shoulder and I flinch at the burst of pain. She draws her hand back, face paling. "Divya, that's Arreth," she says. "Hannah's gone." Then she adds softly, "Arreth's gone too."

My feverish mind takes her words in but refuses to process them. My hands are glowing faintly. They feel stronger now, maybe from the magic—the *too-late* magic. I bring them to your cheeks, try to press my fingers to your face. "Hannah, wait," I say, my voice fading. "I can bring you back..."

You don't move. And then the last of my strength is gone, and I slump back, exhausted beyond words. Milly puts a life jacket behind my head, pulls the blanket back around me, and reaches out to stroke my hair. "It's okay," she says, and her voice follows me down the tunnel to unconsciousness. "Rest now, Divya. You tried..."

~

I WAKE UP. It's night and I'm still in the boat. And Arreth is still dead. Milly rests her fingers on my head; I wonder how long she's been soothing me. Pain rushes back to greet me, along with my old friends horror and grief.

"I didn't try hard enough," I mutter. "Or fast enough."

Milly startles at my voice. "You did all you could, Divya. It's okay."

That's what she's supposed to say. What anyone is supposed to say in a situation like this. It doesn't bring Arreth back. I remember, in my fog of pain and fever, mistaking Arreth for you, which must have been a final insult to Arreth if she could hear me at all.

"I *had* the magic," I say. "You saw it, right?"

Then I knuckle my forehead. No, she's blind—although, wait—

"Yes, I saw it," Milly says. "Like I saw Brooks's magic, and Nadia's. I could see yours. But it wasn't strong enough to save her, and that's not your fault."

I shake my head. I couldn't buy that line when friends tried to console me about losing you. I can't accept it now. Right after we escaped downtown Portsmouth, Nadia did encourage me to practice my magic—if I had any—but I refused. I was afraid of attracting the spiders' attention. When I should have been fearing the locals more...

Ah, Arreth. Ah, Hannah.

I squeeze Milly's hand and give a shuddering sigh. "I... ugh. Thanks for trying to make me feel better. Let's..." I glance at Arreth's body. "Let's talk about something else. Do we—uh, do we know where we're going?"

"She does," Milly says, nodding at Nadia, who hunches over the steering wheel, consulting a nautical map laid out on the seat beside her. "Guess she learned how to pilot a boat growing up... well, you've seen her family's house. Loaded and on the waterfront. Of course they had a boat. It was her idea to grab one after you said the spiders hated seawater. Also—faster than an ATV!"

"But they attacked the Ballroom-two," I say, frowning and thinking back. The scene is fragmented, shot through with memories of pain that aggravate my aches in the present. "They ended up not being afraid of the water underneath the place after all."

"I told them to," Milly says quietly.

I sit up, ignoring the protests from my body. "You *what*?!"

She looks away, though it's not like I can meet her eyes anyway. "I... told them there was a big feast waiting for them in the Ballroom. I told them not to be afraid. That they'd be safe."

"Good god," I mumble. "Hell of a distraction."

"I knew the spiders might get us too," Milly says. "But it —it seemed worth the risk, if they'd kill a bunch of those bastards. Hearing your screams, Divya, I... lost it. I don't regret what I did, but I—man, I'm supposed to *protect* people, not sic monsters on them. Even people I disagree with. What does that say about me, that I don't feel bad about it?"

"Technically you're no longer a cop," I say. "Protecting people isn't your job anymore. And—seriously, *fuck* those fanatics anyway."

"Yeah," she says. "The heck with 'em. They screwed with the wrong women."

She gives me a tiny smile, reminding me of when we were friends, what seems like ages ago. The two Injuns, as the late Ben Ulrich would say: Allard and Fragonard against the evildoers of Portsmouth and the bigots in their own department. Both of us were forced to hang up our badges, but now here we are again together, embarked on something like a righteous mission. If we could recapture even a little of the bond we once had, maybe the multiverse wouldn't seem so dark to me.

"But—how did you talk *back* to the spiders?" I ask. "I knew you could hear them, but..."

"Same way I hear them," she says. "Which is to say, I have absolutely no idea. There is something, though, I neglected to tell you. Back at Nadia's house."

I raise an eyebrow. "Oh?"

"Didn't want you to think I was crazy. Still don't."

I can't help but laugh, though the motion sends shockwaves through me. "You—ugh—you were worried *I* would think *you* were crazy? That's a first. Come on, what is it?"

Milly removes her helmet and rolls it in her lap, playing with it nervously. "I've been... dreaming about spiders. For weeks. Well, *one* spider in particular. I think it's the one you guys keep referring to as 'Bloated Belly.'"

Though I swear she can't hear us over the engine noise, Nadia looks back at us.

"What... what happens in your dreams, usually?" I say. Milly didn't have to worry. I don't think she's crazy at all. But I'm alarmed all the same.

"Not much," she admits. "They, uh, started up not long after I lost my eyes. The big spider talks without its mouth moving, but all it says is that I belong to it. And my time is coming. Stuff that doesn't make sense."

"Bloated... the spider doesn't say *what* the time is coming to do, or what your time is for? Nothing like that?"

"Nah. It's—more like it's been trying to *claim* me. I don't know how to explain it better. But in the dreams, I usually tell it to piss off."

This is strong language for Milly. Clearly these dreams have been upsetting her; I wish she'd felt like she could tell me in the beginning. Maybe I would have chosen for her to stay home after all—I don't want this Bloated Belly thing claiming my friend, whatever that might mean.

"So you've got some connection to it," I say. "Maybe it was triggered by your being in Avariccia for so long. But—I'd think, then, that you'd develop a connection to the Hand That Never Closes instead. Like I do."

Milly nods. She was there in the City of Games—even if she couldn't see it, she could *hear* how I was able to summon a finger of the Hand to crush the Soldier Lord. Though I refrain from mentioning the vision I had of the Hand while dangling from the *strappado*, when it demanded I make a sacrifice of someone else to save myself. *Maybe it chose Arreth*, comes the unbidden thought. But I'm unwilling to consider such a horrible possibility. At least for now...

"Maybe the Hand's not my type," Milly says, half-joking.

If we each have a "type" of magic, might we each also attract a certain type of Port master...?

Life turned to death, and death turned to life.

I shove the notion out of my mind—or Notion, if you will—and fumble for any remaining pieces I'm missing about our escape. The figure with the gun flashes into my mind, viewed upside down as I viewed him then.

"Was it—was it LaPlante-two who shot Arreth?" I ask.

Milly nods grimly. "As soon as the spiders attacked, he was out of there—never mind his 'flock' screaming for his help. The fraud. He must have had the same idea about getting a boat, because he turned up there soon after we did. Pretty ticked at us for ruining his show, I guess. After he shot Arreth, Nadia went for him and..."

She turns her head toward our pilot, cocking an ear. "I never saw anything like it. It was like she had no fear at all, just rage. She broke the preacher's neck. Wrenched his head. Girl is *strong*." Then she lowers her voice and gives me that tiny smile again. "You oughta keep on her good side, Divya."

I ought to. And right now I want to touch her, wrap my arms around her, but I physically can't. Suddenly I remember my realization about LaPlante$_2$'s young acolyte, that he was effectively Nadia's brother. How would it make her feel to know? Did she figure it out already?

Time enough to discuss that later.

Milly leans toward me. "Been meaning to ask you, Divya.

Do you and Nadia, uh... I mean at one point I thought you might be..."

I'm conscious of Arreth's body in the boat with us. Though I'm no longer messed up enough to confuse her with you, I can't abide her looking in my direction with those blank, open eyes. I reach over and gently roll your—her!—lids down. "I don't know," I say. "It's, humm, complicated."

"We're low on fuel," Nadia announces from the front. "I think we've got enough to round the rest of the way around Cape Ann, but after that we're gonna have to find someplace to put ashore."

"And get more fuel?" Milly says.

"Or walk, if we can't find any," Nadia shouts back.

Hmm. I've got my fingers crossed for the fuel. It'd be a hell of a long walk from Gloucester$_2$ to Boston$_2$ if the geography is the same here. I lie back and catch more rest as the boat speeds onward. Nadia's been keeping close to shore the whole time, and I've been seeing scattered lights on land, but this stretch of the peninsula seems dark by comparison. Maybe it got hit hard.

After we clear Cape Ann$_2$, Nadia gives an update: we're running on fumes. I see only darkness on shore. Then I catch an unexpected drift of sound from somewhere ahead of us. Voices. Sounds like they're coming from *on* the water, not ashore. I strain to listen, thinking that at the first mention of the "Protector," I'm out. Instead, I hear a reference to aspirin.

Calm voices, discussing practical matters. It's the most welcoming sound in the world.

"I hear a group of survivors," I tell Nadia. "Probably not even religious crazies. I can guide us there."

"I hope they're close!"

For the next few minutes, I shout out calibrations to Nadia's steering, and we make our way closer to shore, but running mostly parallel to it. Then we spot a bobbing collection of lights out on the water ahead. Boats. Multiple boats. That's where the voices are coming from. Nadia slows the boat.

"One of them said something like 'Wisewoman,'" I holler at her. "Any guesses what that means?"

"Well, it's a—a traditional thing, with a lot of cultures," Nadia answers. "The wise woman is like a shaman."

"So, religion again," I say, bristling.

"Not in the same way," Nadia says. "I think we should give 'em a shot. We're—"

The engine coughs and sputters. The boat slows further, and then the engine dies. We're still distant from the group of boats, but they can probably see our light like we see theirs. I call out to Nadia. "Can you flash your light?"

She blinks it off and on a couple of times. A few minutes pass. Then we notice one of the lights detach itself from the group and become larger. It resolves itself into a small craft carrying two women, approaching us over the dark water. They're visible as little more than silhouettes. One of the women, the smaller one, has a rifle, but the larger one is unarmed; this latter woman is the one who hollers to us across the waves.

"You need help?"

"Yeah," Nadia calls back. "We're out of fuel and we have an injured person on board."

"Where did you come from and where are you going?"

I add my voice to the conversation. "We come from New Hampshire, where a bunch of fanatics almost killed us. They *did* kill one of us; she's here on the boat. You're not anti-magic, are you?"

"Thephal's grace, that sounds awful," the woman answers. "No, we respect and revere magic. But we're not fools, either. Don't make that mistake. Do you have any weapons?"

Nadia replies in the negative. Apparently Jeong's gun is long gone.

"Then follow me," says the woman. "And welcome to Salaam-on-the-Sea."

13

Salaam-on-the-Sea turns out to be a collection of boats and rafts tied together and anchored to the harbor of—yes, Salaam, Massachusetts. The woman corrects my pronunciation when I call it "Salem."

I can't see the city itself in the darkness, but our rescuer, the broad-shouldered, red-haired woman who introduces herself as simply "Tucker," tells us there's not much to look at since the spiders had their way with it.

"All that history, gone," Tucker laments. I'm aboard one of the larger boats, which she referred to as "HMS Morphine." As the name suggests, the boat is outfitted with scrounged medical equipment and a couple cots. Despite their protests, Nadia and Milly have been banished to an adjacent room, where they're rehydrating and eating snacks. Tucker stays with me to await the arrival of two doctors from elsewhere in the survivors' colony.

Scratch that. Even amid the pain lingering from my "resettling," I realize Tucker didn't say doctors were on the way. She said healers.

With my injuries, I'm powerless to do anything even if

this is another wacko cult. So I politely advance the conversation. "Are you—were you—a historian?"

"Of a sort," she says, smiling down at me. "I worked at one of the witchcraft museums. Many of us did. Are you from around here?"

"No."

"Big business in town is—well, was—the tourist industry. But beyond all the silly witch costumes and souvenirs, we prided ourselves on telling the real story of what happened in New England those hundreds of years ago. The true narrative is persecution... I hope I showed visitors that the trials weren't about magic, they were about hate and fear of others."

She pauses. "But—some people still need to learn the lesson, based on what happened to you. You said that preacher called it a *strappado*?"

"Yeah. He was real proud of it."

"Thephal preserve us from madmen. I should have known that we'd all finish each other off before the spiders could get a chance."

A man and a woman enter the room, dressed in the same type of casual clothes that Tucker wears. That's a relief; I might have made a genuine effort at escape if they came in dressed like, er, shamans. "Who's this, Mother?" the man asks my host.

"Dammit, Elliott, I asked you to stop calling me that," Tucker snaps. "It's not funny and it never was."

Mother... Tucker. Oh.

"This is Divya Allard. She's suffering from dislocation of both arms and Thephal knows what else. She's been through hell." Tucker folds her own arms over her belly. "I hope you're both rested up and ready to work?"

"Of course," says the woman. She's short and in her late

forties or early fifties, with a kind face. "Divya, I'm Elthaba. Have you ever received healing before?"

"I—what? Yeah, I mean, I've been to the hospital. I have a primary."

Then I realize what she's referring to. Elthaba and Elliott must be "creeps." Like me, but effective. "No, I guess not," I correct myself.

"It will feel strange. It will hurt. A lot. Do you trust that we're not here ultimately to harm you, though?"

I give her a weak nod. "Okay."

And then they begin. I understand immediately why Tucker insisted that my friends go to a different room. My screams are almost as bad as when my body was being broken in the first place. Tucker hurries out of the room to go placate Nadia and Milly.

With Elthaba and Elliott's glowing hands on me (glowing far more brightly than my own did when I failed to heal Arreth), I can feel my tissue reknitting, my bones regluing, my bruises fading, but it's far from a comforting sensation. More like someone is tying and retying knots inside me. My arms pop back into place and that earns my loudest shriek. Toward the end of the healing, Elliott's hands concentrate solely on my forehead, as if to soothe my brain itself.

I take a deep breath and my body stops trying to fold itself together. I lie back, letting the messy business of healing do its work, and close my eyes.

When I open them again, I see that Nadia and Milly have entered the room, both looking concerned. I smile wide at them to put their minds at ease, or at least Nadia's. "It was good for me, good for them, good for all of us."

"How do you... feel?" Nadia asks.

"I..." I flex an arm. "Wow!" My limb responds in a

delightfully normal way, with no pain attending the action. I sit up on the cot. I feel no pain at all; I feel better than my baseline, in fact. I look around for Elthaba and Elliott, to thank them, but they're gone. Tucker remains, however, her feet propped up on a chair in the corner.

"You'll crash later," Tucker says. "After all the discomfort involved in the actual process, the healing gives you a temporary high. But—yeah, you're good now. Any more serious injury and my people might have been outmatched, but you were just the right amount of broken."

"Thanks!" I say. "I have to ask, though... how the hell did Elliott and Elthaba get so *good* at what they do? I thought most people could only produce dollar magic in this world."

Nadia shoots me a warning glance as Tucker says, "Uh, what? This world?"

"This area, she means," Nadia says. "She's not from around here."

"Ah," says the red-haired woman. "Well, Divya, if you're up for a stroll, I can introduce you to a few of my friends. They're eager to meet any new survivors, and they've already talked the ears off Nadia and Milly. What do you say?"

There's pink light coming through the window of the room. Daybreak. I jump out of the bed, but not because I'm excited for a tour of Salaam-on-the-Sea. "Shit," I say. "Shit! How many hours have gone by? I don't know if Ethan's been able to hold out this long."

"Ethan?" Tucker asks, furrowing her brow. I realize yet again that I can't keep my mouth shut. Side effect of that freaky healing, I guess, but that doesn't mean I can stop it.

I pace the length of the room, shaking my head. "We can't—we have to—shit, we have to get down to Boston-two ASAP!"

"Divya," Nadia says in a despairing tone.

"Can I please borrow her for a few minutes?" Tucker asks her—not me. "I hope this healing has demonstrated our goodwill. I mean to... there are things I'd like to know. I won't ask anything that's unfair, but I consider a few questions to be a bargain for the level of healing Divya has received."

Nadia looks ready to refuse anyway. But she slumps her shoulders and says, "Sure. Give her a break if she gets too riled up, though... Mother."

Tucker throws her a half-snarl. "I'm going to kill that Elliott." She turns to me. "Come on, Divya, would you like a bite to eat as well?"

I feel like I'm ready to bounce off the walls—open air sounds like a fine idea. I walk out with the woman to the deck of the boat. Dawn is breaking over Salaam-on-the-Sea. I see a number of people out on the other boats or sitting on the rafts strung between them.

"Nobody looks like a witch," I observe. "Not a floppy hat in sight."

"We Wisewomen have a strong distaste for cliché," Tucker admits.

"Can you tell me how you improved your magic? Was it practice? Ten thousand hours or whatever? I tried healing, myself, but I *sucked*." I take a breath and realize I've given too much away.

Tucker wears a knowing smile. "I thought I'd get to ask the questions. Permit me a few, please, and then I can enlighten you further. You let slip that you're from another world. I already suspected as much from talking to your friends... either you three intelligent young women have been living in a cave for most of your lives, or you *are* not from around here in a planetary sense. Can you come clean with me?"

Well, the Wisewomen have already done a lot for me. And my tongue is still loose.

"We're from an alternate version of this world," I say. "With no magic. To me, this is all 'two'… Salaam-two, Boston-two, even 'two' versions of people that I know back home. We don't belong here."

"Then why *are* you here?"

"To help a friend. Well, a murderous former enemy. It's a long story—but we need to get to a place in Boston-two… your Boston, that is… that is tied together in an important way in our world." I don't have the patience to explain biplanar locks. I'm starting to feel like I've already lost her. Then again, I am talking super fast. I skid to a halt and jump back a conversational pace. "So you *do* believe we're from another world?"

"Number one," says Tucker, "my friends and I believe a lot of stuff mainstream folks would dismiss out of hand. Number two, mutant spiders have destroyed my world, so I'd be a fool *not* to expand my, ahem, worldview as a result. But I have a pet theory, which I hope you'll indulge, that item two is not unrelated to your arrival from this alternate world."

I go to the railing. The waft of someone cooking eggs on a nearby vessel reaches my nostrils. "Where's that breakfast you were talking about?"

"Contingent upon your honest responses," says the red-haired woman, shrugging. "Sorry to impose a condition *post facto*. So help me out. Are you in any way responsible for the mysterious arrival of these world-ending spiders?"

I can take that *you* any number of ways, to be perfectly academic—and academic distinctions are fair when talking to a person who casually throws out the phrase "*post facto*." I interpret her question as being directed only to me, not to the entirety of our trio of castaways. "No. In fact, I'd like to help get rid of them if at all possible."

"Good," Tucker says. "I like a dimensional traveler who doesn't hold onto a provincial sense of responsibility. We are all one, et cetera. And I would prefer not to live on a boat for the rest of my life. So, next question. Have you, in your travels, encountered a pregnant woman riding one of the spiders like she'd tamed it?"

My mouth drops open.

"I haven't seen this... person," the Wisewoman goes on. "But one of my colleagues did—shortly before we fled Salaam and got the idea to put the boat colony together. She told me what she saw, and I'm inclined to take her at her word."

"Is she here? Your colleague, I mean?"

Tucker shakes her head. "Didn't make it."

"I'm sorry."

I couldn't hide my surprise at hearing the same mythological-sounding figure that Father LaPlante$_2$ described. A woman as sharp as Tucker wouldn't miss the recognition on my face. Still, she puts me to the test. "Have you seen such a person? Riding a spider?"

"No." Here I can add some honest clarification, in case Tucker is considering keelhauling us after all. "But the fanatical preacher who tortured me—he told his congregation he had a religious 'vision' of a pregnant woman on a spider. He must have literally seen her, same as your late friend did."

"Could this unlikely creature have come from your world too?"

"It's possible," I admit. "But I have no idea who she would be."

Tucker nods, seemingly satisfied. "All right, let's cross over to the chow boat. And then, I believe, we have a burial at sea to perform."

Arreth. "Oh, no, we don't have time to—"

"I must insist," she says firmly. "Your friend's soul will have a lonely journey of it otherwise."

I manage to nod and look abashed, though my foot is seized by urgent tapping.

The Wisewoman adds, in a gentler tone, "You may also want to make *time* for one other item before you leave on your rescue mission. You mentioned you have the ability to heal, but that it 'sucks,' I think you said. Elthaba and Elliott would, I'm sure, be willing to share some advice on that front…"

∽

AT THE END of my lesson with the two healers, I look at the rising sun in the sky. I hope the hour I spent learning to concentrate intention and growth in my hands didn't tank the mission.

We let the Wisewomen of Salaam-on-the-Sea perform a rite to consign Arreth's remains to the Atlantic. They've performed the same rite for a number of their friends and colleagues. Tucker, the putative group leader if not its "mother," sing-speaks as they lower Arreth's cloth-wrapped body into the waves:

"*Blessed Thephal, in your infinite wisdom and compassion*
Grace this soul's passage with the company of your Owl
And let Arreth Ryder find peace and enlightenment
In the glades and gardens of Fath the Giver, for all time."

The other Wisewomen murmur in response, "So mote it be." Then Arreth is gone from this world, and I hope on her way to the next—to *some* next, anyway, that's kinder than this one.

Tucker and her friends gas up our stolen boat. They give us a few supplies and some words of advice about our destination as the sun reaches its zenith.

"We have been improving our magic through practice, over time, with Thephal's wisdom always centered in our minds," Tucker says. "Boston—the so-called City of Notions—takes an entirely different approach to wielding magic. Being from another world, you won't have heard of the Brahmin Project."

We shake our heads.

"Damn," says the Wisewoman Elliott. "Are you *sure* you need to go down there?"

"Yes, we're idiots, we've established that," I say. "So—what is this Brahmin Project? I know the word from a different context... it's one of the castes in the country where I was born, India."

"It is in our world's India too," Tucker says. "The highest caste, yes? Well, the 'high-caste' folks in Boston—the richest and the most politically connected—gave themselves the same nickname. But the Boston Brahmins weren't content to have the most money, land, power, etc. They also wanted to have the best magic. So for many generations they've been breeding potent magicians in their small circle of families with each other, though there's no evidence of higher magic effectiveness being a heritable trait. Training and practicing is the only proven way of increasing magic power."

"Then why would they keep doing it—the Brahmin Project—if breeding magic doesn't work?"

The red-haired woman gives me a cynical smile. "You've heard the story of the tsar's new clothes?"

"Er, emperor, but yeah, close enough."

"What do you think the hangers-on around the Brahmins keep telling them? 'No, I don't see any measurable difference in your magic,' or 'Sir, you are the most powerful magician I've ever met'? Reality distortion isn't just a spell, Divya my dear."

Nadia smiles.

"Now, don't get me wrong," Tucker goes on, "all that self-importance has yielded some useful advancements for society at large over the years. The Bostonians call them Notions: ideas for progressing civilization. Equal rights for women is one. Leveling the playing field for historically oppressed peoples, such as Arreth's ancestors, that's another Notion. Championing the arts and sciences as instruments of Fath's will is another. But, blinded by a belief in their own significance, the Boston Brahmins have long forgotten the original context in which Boston was nicknamed the 'City of Notions.'"

Milly and I look at each other blankly. Nadia, however, straightens up. The enlightenment dawning on her features makes them even finer. "Notions has another definition," she says.

Tucker grins down at her. "Very good, kid. You did strike me as the brightest in your bunch. Yes, in an older sense, 'notions' refers to small items for sale, particularly related to sewing and other crafts: buttons, ribbons, thread, and so forth. One source I'm familiar with defines them as 'trifling in size and value.' So what I want you to remember is that our Boston wasn't defined by grand ideas and innovations after all—'City of Notions' actually means people saw it as a giant *department store.*"

Our boat bobs on the waves. Tucker has spent a good deal of time taking the proverbial wind out of our sails.

"Why are you telling us all this?" I say.

"I want you to be prepared," Tucker says. "Ideas and delusions mean nothing to big, hungry, killer spiders. When you get to Boston, you will in all probability find that everyone there is dead."

14

We motor away from Salaam-on-the-Sea infected by Tucker's gloomy prophecy for Boston$_2$. Which matches exactly with what Father LaPlante$_2$ told us to expect in the City of Notions, though for different reasons. I haven't been expecting to reunite with anyone in Boston$_2$, but a thoroughly flattened and spider-haunted city will be especially difficult to cross if we want to reach the FBI field office in one piece.

I break the silence by saying, "Mother Tucker heard about a pregnant woman riding a spider. LaPlante-two supposedly had a vision of the same thing. That *couldn't* be anyone from the Portwalkers, right? Do you have any pregnant members?"

Nadia, at the wheel once again, lets out a puff of air, as if she's been holding her breath since we left Salaam-on-the-Sea. "No. I mean, I don't think so. I haven't seen anyone with a, a..."

"Bloated belly," Milly suggests.

The coincidence of phrasing disturbs me in a profound way, though I can't exactly say why. I take a stab at it. "This

—Bloated Belly, Fifty Furred Limbs, that was its whole name, right? It's aligned with earth... what about, like, fertility?"

Nadia grunts. "Yeah. I think so. So—maybe someone who's been knocked up would make for an ideal emissary. But... hmm. *Why* would a person unleash a bunch of monster spiders into this world? What kind of horrible villain would do that? And how would they get on the spiders' *side* in the first place?"

By now in my adventures, I can imagine a hundred different self-justifications that would permit a person to destroy a world. If I were to write a thesis, it would be this: People are shit. But the question of how someone would ally themselves with the monsters is a good one. Perhaps someone with a direct line to Bloated Belly itself. Like I, for better or worse, seem to have developed with the Hand That Never Closes.

But the only person I know to have such a connection is Milly herself, here in this boat with us and obviously neither pregnant nor riding a spider. And I dragged her here.

"How many earth Ports have you and your Portwalker friends stumbled across so far?" I ask Nadia, leaning forward.

"Divya, you know I can't tell you that." She mimes strangling herself.

"Awfully goddamn convenient."

She glances back at me, clearly hurt. "I wish I could tell you. But I can process whatever you need me to process, if you explain yourself."

"I'm guessing you have no records of who's gone where, and when."

"We intentionally don't keep track of that, because—"

"—because you're not their boss. It's an autonomous collective. Blah blah. Yeah. But consider, if you knew who'd visited an earth Port recently, you could track the cross-contamination. I mean... they wouldn't be able to summon the spiders, or Bloated Belly itself, from *our* world, right? It must have originated from one of Bloated Belly's turf worlds."

"Right."

I purse my lips, thinking through another angle of the mystery. "We can rule out all the dudes. That cuts down our suspect pool by half, yeah?"

"Less than half, but yeah, of course."

Chicks dig Portwalking. "That leaves X number of women —only you know the number. Now throw out all the women past childbearing age. How does that narrow our pool?"

"By about another third. But, Allard, none of them were pregnant when—"

"Are there any you haven't seen in a while?"

"Not for more than a few weeks," Nadia says.

"Have you ever run across a Port in which *time* runs differently than in our world? Like, it could run several months there while only a couple of weeks pass back home?"

She's slow to answer. "Once. But time ran slower there, not faster—a minute there would make an hour go by on Earth. And it wasn't an earth Port."

"But that means a time differential *is* possible."

She doesn't respond.

I'm getting excited. Not as excited as the Wisewomen's healing magic made me, but close. "Rule out every youngish woman you've seen in the past week or so—the spiders arrived in this world at least a week ago. How many women of childbearing age does that leave?"

"Five."

"*Five!* That's great. Now how many of them have spider-riding skills? Trained on a pony, maybe?"

"Allard, this isn't funny," Nadia snaps back. "Besides—what does it matter who did this? I don't see how it can possibly be undone, even if we do identify the culprit!"

"We have to try," Milly speaks up. "You both made a promise to Arreth, and you can't take it back now."

The skyline of Boston$_2$ comes into view on the horizon, and all three of us fall quiet at the sight of it. Tucker was right. LaPlante$_2$ was right. The city has been devastated. Many of the skyscrapers are toppled or listing dangerously, including the iconic glass-walled Hancock Tower$_2$, which has fallen on the church beneath it in Copley Square$_2$, all of its striking surface shattered. The only recognizable tower remaining upright is the blocky Prudential$_2$, and there's a fire burning on top.

It hits me like a fist to the chest. Sorrow, grief, the deepest despair. They warned us, but we had to see the ruin for ourselves. There'll be nothing left to unlock in Back Bay$_2$. Our mission is doomed, and we've got no way to get home, either, with the spiders likely having leveled Portsmouth$_2$ by now. Tears stream down my face.

"It's gone," I say. "Boston-two is gone."

I look over at Milly. She has no eyes with which to cry, but her lip is trembling. The boat slows, and I see Nadia's shoulders shaking. I hear her sob loudly.

We should throw ourselves into the ocean. Sink under the waves. It'd be better than ending up in a spider's belly. We should sink this goddamn boat. Nadia turns off the engine altogether, as if the same possibility has occurred to her.

"It's over," she cries. "It's all over."

"Wait," says Milly. "There's still hope. We need to check it out."

"What's the point?" I groan. "We're fucked. We might as well kill ourselves."

"A-agreed," Nadia says, sobbing.

"Hey. Hey!" Milly stands up in the boat, rocking it perilously. "What the... ugh. What the heck has gotten into you two? Isn't it early to throw in the towel? I've come all this way, with only this frigging helmet to help me get by, and I think—"

Then she stops. I glance up at her, sniveling, barely able to focus through the overwhelming wave of suicidal angst. Milly stands still, swiveling her head toward Boston$_2$ even without the aid of vision. Then she says:

"Magic. Should've known. I see it now. And holy cow, it's strong. So strong to reach us all the way out here."

I wave a hand at her. "Who cares if there's magic or not." I stare over the side at the dark depths of the Atlantic$_2$. What a relief oblivion would be, to escape this crushing despair.

Milly grabs my dismissive hand, holding my wrist tightly enough to grind the bones together. As I cry out in pain, she belts me across the face with the other hand, doubling the number of bright stars exploding before my eyes.

"Heartburners," she hisses. "I'll try to block it."

Milly lets go and concentrates. Momentarily stunned out of my false despair, I blink at her. "Shit."

I launch myself forward and grab Nadia by the waist. She's gotten one leg over the side of the boat. She looks like I've betrayed her by stopping her from jumping into the ocean.

"You'll never feel for me what you felt for her," she mutters, trying to pry my hands off her. "I saw Arreth shatter you all over again."

That hurts. And the temporary pain Milly gifted me with is fading, bringing the heartburners' despair magic back. My hands loosen on their own.

Then—both Nadia and I gasp as the heavy weight of emotional manipulation lifts. I see Milly standing with her arms folded; she gives me a bare nod.

"I'm blocking it from all three of us," she says. "But I can't do it for long. Go! Get this boat going again!"

Nadia flutters her lashes, looking down at herself. She hoists her leg back into the boat and I let her go. She gives me a haunted look. "Divya, I—"

"Start it up!" I holler. "Please!"

She guns the engine. The boat roars toward the ruined city. Milly sways and I help her into a seated position; her arms remain crossed. Man, I hope she can hold out for a few minutes, or else I can see Nadia driving us right into a pier...

As the wind streams my hair behind me in a black torrent and the wreck of Boston$_2$ looms larger, I think: *Magic. That means people. People who don't want us getting near...*

So there are a few survivors after all—with incredibly powerful magic at their disposal. Tucker was wrong on that count. She might be wrong about a few other things too. We don't know what we're plowing into. The buildings along the seaport become visible, shattered like all the rest. The masts of sunken boats are sticking out of the harbor. I see half of "Old Ironsides," the U.S.S. Constitution, submerged to our right.

Wrecked boats and ships.

How did the spiders wreck them, if the stupid old creatures are afraid of seawater?

I don't want to ask Milly and disrupt her concentration. Sweat pours down her face, streaking down the smooth flesh where her eyes used to be, despite the cold winds whipping up from the waves. But maybe I already know the answer.

"I could make for the mouth of the Charles," Nadia shouts suddenly. "We could take the river all the way to Back Bay."

I look further inland and I spot it before she does: the Zakim Bridge[2] has collapsed into the river, blocking it up. Right now I'm not sure what's real and what's not, but I'd rather not take the chance. "No go," I say. "Dock at the seaport."

Milly's concentration, or will, or both, breaks as we're coming to a long dock. As soon as she exhales, wiping her forehead, I feel the hammer of the unseen heartburners striking me again, and I physically stagger. "Not this time," I mutter. "Not this time! Fight it, Nadia!"

"Goddammit," she moans, letting up on the wheel.

The boat is going too fast as we pull up alongside the dock. The wreck of someone's yacht is dead ahead.

Who cares? Death is going to be welc—

"Slow it down!" I yell. "*STOP!*"

Nadia shrieks and grabs the wheel, doubling over it as if fighting herself from the inside out. She kills most of our momentum, but not enough to stop us from striking the overturned yacht—

And we pass right through it.

Somehow we're *inside* the yacht as the boat finally stops. Milly says between ragged breaths, "What—happened? Are we—dead?"

"Far from it," I say. "Our obstacle was a lie. And I have a feeling there are more lies ahead. Milly, are you out of juice? Can you see the magic around us?"

"I don't need much to see it..." She tilts her head, "looks" around, and makes a clucking sound. "Wow. We're past the field of despair they're casting, but... there's *so* much more magic here. The mind—mind-effers. They're sustaining..."

"A city-sized illusion," I say. I knew it in my gut, and I know it now, though we're surrounded by the lie.

Boston$_2$ isn't ruined at all. But dozens, if not hundreds, of mindfuckers are laboring to make it look that way.

∼

I CAN REMEMBER the last time you and I went to Boston. It was at your insistence, as I recall. You wanted the dumb policewoman to get out of our little Podunk for a night and get some real big-city *Culture*. Driving and parking was a nightmare. We caught a musical at the Opera House and had an amazing meal of dumplings and spicy noodles in Chinatown.

As we were walking around the streets afterward, you saw a homeless man and his dog huddled together on a blanket. You went over, pressed a twenty into his hand that you couldn't afford to give away (dinner and the *theatah* were on me, remember?), and you said, "*Don't give up. There are whole worlds beyond this.*"

At the time I thought you were speaking in a New Age sense—or else trying to motivate him, albeit in a horrible, pull-up-by-the-bootstraps fashion. I didn't ask for clarification. It's one of the many things you said that I've had the occasion to roll around in my head, over and over, ever since I learned you were a member of Nadia's cult. That you were a Portwalker.

The clues were all around me. But I didn't even know, or care, that I had a mystery to solve.

As we pass by a seemingly decimated South Station$_2$

and through the business district, stepping over junk that isn't there and then tripping over invisible obstacles that *are* there, the illusion fades. Milly mutters that it must be limited to the outer perimeter of the city, a defense mechanism just like the field of despair set up by the heartburners.

So we see the city as it really is.

I pay only scant attention to the cosmetic differences between Boston$_2$ and the Boston I know—the crescent moons factoring into so many building motifs, the big light-up sign near Fenway Park featuring a staring eye and something called "Zipper Cola" instead of the Citgo triangle, etc. Instead I focus on the obstacles between us and Back Bay$_2$ and the end of my mission.

And Boston$_2$, in reality, hasn't been touched much by the spiders at all. There are broken streets here and there, evidence of scattered attacks, but nothing like the wholesale devastation that the hidden defenders of the city would have us believe.

However, corpses line the streets, out of proportion with the amount of actual property damage. It's a terrible sight—I've never seen so many bodies in one place. Everything is still, with no sign of the living. I kneel by several specimens as we head down Summer Street$_2$, Nadia looking green and turning away, Milly giving a few wretched sniffs before making a conscious effort to block her nostrils.

Many of the corpses look curiously withered, like mummies unwrapped from their bandages; that's not an effect I've seen any spiders leave behind. Others have been bludgeoned or shot to death, not ripped apart or half-eaten.

I stick close to my companions as Summer$_2$ turns to Winter$_2$ and we approach the intersection with Tremont Street$_2$. "I don't think spiders killed these people," I say. "Or at least not most of them."

"Who do you suppose did?" Milly asks.

"There's been a lot of effort to keep visitors out of the city—I'm guessing the same people are responsible." I peer ahead, across the street to Boston Common$_2$, where I glimpse the first breathing locals. Dozens are clumped together sitting cross-legged in the park.

"Stop," I say, throwing my arm in front of my companions. "Don't let them see us."

We flatten ourselves against a storefront advertising the very best in proven magical enhancements, peering past a used music and game shop to the crowd on the Common$_2$. I notice now that most of them have their eyes closed, so they wouldn't have spotted us anyway.

"Mind-effers," Milly says.

I suppress a hysterical laugh at her reluctance to use the "F" word even at a time like this. "The ones maintaining the illusion around the city?"

"Yeah," she says, the wonder plain in her voice. "They're working *together* somehow, combining their similar magic into an absolutely massive force."

"Tucker underestimated the Brahmins," Nadia says. "Or else these aren't Brahmins at all, but a totally different approach. A democratic approach, even."

"Doesn't mean they're nice people," I warn. "Don't forget about all the damn bodies in the street."

"I'm sensing one peeling off. Coming our way." Milly tenses. "I'm sorry, I don't have the energy to protect us if he or she tries to mess with our minds."

I lost Ethan's Glock to the New Church of Fath, so I'll have to defend us the old-fashioned way. I pick up a piece of rebar from the street and wield it like a club. "If it's one, I can take them on."

Then I see who's walking across Park Street: a well-muscled Asian-American man in his thirties, dressed much differently than I'm used to, in a wild striped shirt and cargo shorts. It's definitely him, though. He's carrying a Springfield M1A rifle and wearing a grim expression.

There's no hiding from him. As he meets my eyes, I exclaim: "Jeong!"

The man stops. Points his rifle at us. "Who the fuck are you, and how do you know me?"

15

Okay, it's not Ethan Jeong. For a second, I let the welcome sight of someone who looks exactly like my friend overwhelm me. Now "Ethan" sounds like a name from the Bible, so that's probably not his first name here—better stick to "Jeong" for this Jeong$_2$. Better not assume he's a great guy, either.

"What's important is that we're not here to hurt you, any of you," I tell him. "We took a boat in and we're just passing through."

"Passing *through*? To where?!"

"Back Bay," I say. "Then we'll be out of your hair." Except, of course, we may not be—I have no idea how we're going to get home even if we do manage to destroy the biplanar locks.

"Right," Jeong$_2$ says scornfully, stepping closer. "And you're not going to hurt anyone, even though you're clutching a piece of rebar like you want to bash my brains out."

"You have an M<small>IA</small>. I don't think it'd be a fair contest."

But to show my good intentions, I drop the rebar. Jeong$_2$ doesn't lower his rifle.

"Mr. Jeong," Nadia puts in, "I know you must have been through a lot of trauma. It's hard to sort friends from enemies at a time like this. But we're three harmless travelers trying to help out a friend who's—trapped—in a facility in Back Bay. You can point that thing at us the whole time, but let—"

"Quiet," Jeong$_2$ commands her. "I'm talking to the Indian woman. Who hasn't explained how you people know my name."

How stupid of me to have shouted it out. Now I don't know what to tell him. "I know a person... a lot like you," I say. "Ethan Jeong. Works for the FBI. But I see my mistake now, because I'm assuming you don't."

"The FBI?" Jeong$_2$ says. "Would never get in. And my name's not Ethan, it's Dae-seong. So you've definitely got the wrong guy, but you didn't just *wander* into Boston, and you can't be harmless if you managed to get past the Lowell Corps's gauntlet. I don't have time to sort it out—I got word of a problem that needs backup—so the quickest solution would be to shoot you all where you stand."

"*No*," Nadia says, "the quickest thing would be to let us go!"

"I told you to shut up," he snarls at her. "This isn't a group discussion." He points his rifle at her, as if she'll be the first one to eat a bullet.

Think. Think. If this Jeong$_2$ is anything like Jeong, he's conditioned himself to make hard choices for what he thinks is the greater good. Right now we don't fit into that greater good.

"We can help you with your problem," I blurt out. Then

I make a not-so-wild guess. "A pregnant woman riding a spider. Am I right?!"

He lowers the rifle, staring at me. "Yeah. Friend of yours?"

"No, no, definitely not. We're here to stop her."

"I thought you were here to help someone in Back Bay!"

I take a deep breath. *Act like we've already got the job.* "It's all related. Listen, I'm Officer Divya Allard. You already recognized we're no slouches when it comes to magic. And you're gonna need all the help you can get with this spider-woman, if she was able to breach your defenses. Where is she?"

"In Copley Square. Holmes Corps Black is stationed there."

I have no idea what "Holmes Corps Black" is, but I give him a confident nod and say, "Okay, let's go. You can explain more on the way."

"*You* can explain more on the way!" Jeong$_2$ says, outraged. But he doesn't raise his gun again. Though he never entered the command chain in this world, he's responding to the authority I project. "Hold on a minute. I've got a call to make."

He gets out a smartphone. The phone rings from the speaker. "*Phalth here, Longfellow Corps.*"

"It's Dae-seong," says Jeong$_2$. "You guys get any visions of a trio of unfamiliar women sneaking in through the financial district?"

"*Fath's balls, I was gonna call you about that. Don't shoot them. We've had at least a couple seers report a vision of help from three strangers in Copley—you know we got a situation there. It's not guaranteed to come true, but—*"

"Thanks, Phalth," Jeong$_2$ cuts her off. "I'll take 'em down there. See if I can make it true." He ends the call and turns to us.

"You'll answer to me. If you don't, then I don't care what the Longfellows say, I'll shoot you. Got it?"

"Yes, sir," I say, giving him a supposed "win" on this point. "You heard him, ladies. Let's move out."

Milly's features wrinkle, but she follows the sound of my voice, her helmet pinging her around obstacles. Nadia falls in too; she doesn't look confused at all. She looks, in fact, absolutely in love with me.

We hurry down the sidewalk bordering the Common$_2$, which I can see now is loaded with hundreds of cross-legged mindfuckers, all concentrating on maintaining the illusion around the city. Periodically an armed guard like Jeong$_2$ is stationed to defend them. Jeong$_2$ gives the guards a wave as we pass by.

"Who are your friends?" he asks me as we walk south.

"Officer Milly Fragonard, and—er—Special Consultant Nadia Chopin."

"Well, this is the Emerson Corps. And the Lowell Corps is up there; my sister's in charge." Jeong points to the top of the Prudential$_2$, which is certainly not on fire here in reality. A few tiny shapes move on the roof of the skyscraper. "She would be displeased to know you three didn't commit suicide on the way here."

"Oh, it was fine magic," I assure him. "But we happened to have an extremely powerful blocker. Officer Fragonard is one of the best. Now—I assume the Longfellow Corps consists of know-it-alls? The ones who can see into the future or past?"

"Yeah," he says. He stops by a car parked illegally, jutting out into the street. "Get in." He indicates the driver's seat for me.

We get in. I get behind the wheel. Jeong$_2$ rides next to me with his Springfield M1A in his lap.

Going by Jeong$_2$'s directions, I drive the car down Tremont Street$_2$ and turn the wrong way down Bolyston$_2$, encountering no traffic and no pedestrians along the way. I glance at the brownstones flying by, the empty green spaces and streets. "Has *everyone* been press-ganged into one of your corps?" I ask him.

"Everyone that's left," he says. "There were some who resisted. Like the Reformers."

He doesn't need to fill in what happened to them. I already saw the bodies. "No space for conscientious objectors, huh? What about anybody who thought that magic might endanger your city, not protect it?"

"They're not concerned anymore," Jeong$_2$ says with a casualness that chills me to the bone.

Despite my reservations, I have to ask more, have to know more. "Are you Brahmins?"

"Do I look like a Brahmin?" he says.

"No. Wrong skin color."

"You too," he says, and laughs. "At least for the Boston version. No, the Brahmin Project had the right idea, that we needed to strengthen our magic, but the wrong approach. They turned down their noses at the power of the people. A bunch of us realized eventually that we could combine our powers by tapping into an idea from someone that the Brahmins themselves revered. Gaff Waldo Emerson, the namesake for my corps. We needed to form an 'over-soul.'"

"One for each of the magic types," Nadia ventures from the back seat.

For once, Jeong$_2$ doesn't rebuke her for talking. "Right. And we were working on this long *before* the spiders arrived. When they showed up, it was like a sign from Fath that we'd been doing the right thing. We could protect our city from the spiders while everywhere else fell."

"But they eat magic," I say. "The more you use, the more tempting a banquet you make for them. How did you *stop* them?"

"*Magic!*" Jeong$_2$ exclaims, pounding the dashboard so hard I expect his airbag to pop out. "The illusions are to keep human raiders out, but the Lowell Corps can make *spiders* feel suicidal too. And for those that do slip past and make it inside, the Longfellows can see them coming. And then that's where Holmes Corps Black comes in."

We're heading past the still-intact shining Hancock Building$_2$ and the Trinity Church—no, some temple of Fath adorned with a crescent—in the tower's shadow. As we approach the great granite Boston Public Library$_2$, Jeong$_2$ says, "There. Stop there, in front of the library! Stop there!"

"All right, all right," I say, and I put on the brake. I haven't even turned off the car before Jeong$_2$ busts open his door and runs toward the library, his semi-automatic swinging at his side. I notice that unlike most of the other buildings in the city, the library is severely damaged. There's a big ragged hole punched through the roof. Jeong$_2$ keeps looking up at the hole as he runs.

"Hey! Wait up!" I call after him, tumbling out the driver's door. "What's the big hurry?"

"Have to check on Fath!" he shouts back. Or at least that's what it sounds like. But of course that doesn't make sense... Fath is their big invisible guy in the sky. It can't be *in* the library—can it?

My friends get out of the car too. With Jeong$_2$ occupied, this would be a great time to make a break for it and finish the mission we're here for. I turn to them and a resigned look passes among us.

"Dammit," says Nadia. "I wish we could break a promise for once. Steal this damn car and drive it right to the FBI office." She looks at me with her intense green eyes. "But... that's not what we're all about, is it? Or at least not you two."

"You wouldn't abandon them either, if there's something we can do to help," I say. "You didn't abandon me."

"You're different," she says softly. Then she sighs. "But you're right. Let's go."

"I don't *like* this Ethan," Milly says as the three of us hurry toward the library.

I remember vaguely what the BPL looks like in my Boston, enough to note some crucial differences. The BPL_2 still looks like a Renaissance palace with a seventies-style wing jammed onto its side, but the motifs are different: crescents and staring eyes can be found everywhere amid the iron lamps and arched windows.

A few people are stationed on the wide stone steps in front of the building that $Jeong_2$ ascended. They're physically unarmed, but if they belong to this Holmes Corps Black, they still have the ability to harm us with magic. But they wave us on—they too must have gotten the memo from the Longfellow Corps that we'd play a helpful role.

"Holmes Corps Black," I say as soon as we're past them and into the lobby, suddenly getting it. "The creeps. The creeps who can harm, as opposed to the creeps who can heal—I assume they're Holmes Corps White?"

"Yeah, that sounds about right," Nadia says absently, shouldering her way ahead of me. The book scanning gates are unmanned. She comes into an open chamber flanked by stairs and says, "Check out the artwork in here!"

I catch up with her and stop. The central branch of the Boston Public Library in my world has wonderful baroque-style murals and marble and bronze statuary depicting lions, muses, the Holy Grail, etc. Here in the BPL$_2$, the aesthetics are similarly soaring, but they tell stories I'm only beginning to become familiar with. I see that crescent-shaped bundle of wind Arreth identified as Fath, bestowing five types of magic to worshipful humans below. Turning them into creeps, know-it-alls, mindfuckers, heartburners, and blockers. Yes, five, not six, since everyone here regards healers and harmers as two sides of the same creep coin. That number, *five*, makes me more suspicious than ever about this Fath character, whom Nadia named a fraud.

Humans are portrayed using their magical gifts, in turn, to advance society. Thus the birth of great Notions, which are enumerated in the murals too. Arts and sciences flourish, the causes of justice and equality grow less imperfect, wisdom is cherished, learning is paramount. (Clearly these murals and statues were created by believers in Fath the Giver, not LaPlante$_2$ and company's Fath the Asshole.) All sounds great. Too perfect. This Fath takes the credit for all the positive things to come out of civilization, but not for any of the bad stuff...

Jeong$_2$ isn't here. He's gone up the ivory grey steps in the grand staircase, and so we climb them too to look for him. We arrive in the reading room and stop dead.

I remember this room from the library in my world—Bates Hall, though it's probably called something else here. It was majestic there and it is here too, with a barrel-vaulted ceiling at least fifty feet high filled with a motif of sunken panels, and high arched windows lining the hall. Green-shaded banker's lamps top the many tables lining the hall, but no one sits at them now. Instead, dozens of people crowd the center of the reading room and its focal point: a gigantic marble statue, almost as high as the stone ceiling itself, illuminated by sunlight streaming from a giant hole punched through the roof. I recognize the statue as the prophet Thephal, the figure I saw in multiple sand sculptures at Hampton Beach$_2$. She's holding a weighty tome in one hand, and in the other, a crescent-shaped mirror fitted with actual mirror glass. An owl perches on her shoulder. The glass of the mirror is cracked—no, not just the mirror, the entire statue too. From the cracks in the marble, air is gushing out.

But there's something inside the cracks, too. Multiple things, moving, swiveling. As I get closer, I'm horrified to realize that *eyes* are looking out from the fissures all over the statue: multiply shaped and sized eyes, with all the iris colors of the rainbow. Only a few resemble human eyes; the others are almost painful to look at, especially when they look *back* at me.

The people form a loose ring around the statue, all of them facing outward. If this is Holmes Corps Black, then they've been working overtime on their assault magic; many of them are drooping, sweating and tired. Jeong2 stands inside their circle, looking up at the big hole in the ceiling.

"...don't understand how you couldn't stop it, Ropha! Before it did *that!*" he's currently barking at one of the HCB troops, a tall Latina woman in business dress.

"Sorry, dude—it was relentless," she answers him. "We only managed to drive it back. And it *will* be back. We need reinforcements."

"There are no reinforcements, Fath damn it!"

The woman looks up at the statue and then snaps back at Jeong$_2$: "Maybe you shouldn't talk like that in here."

His eyes widen and he drops to his knees before the statue. "Please, I ask for your forgiveness, Fath. I am only concerned for your safety. If you have any guidance..."

"What *is* that thing?" I say, my voice echoing louder than

I intended as I walk in with Nadia and Milly. "Don't tell me *that's* Fath, after all this!"

Twenty or thirty hostile faces swivel toward me, including the reddening face of Jeong$_2$. Air—no, *wind*—gusts violently out of the statue. I guess I could have been more diplomatic in my phrasing, but at this point I'm too weary and wrung out to care. Jeong$_2$ gets to his feet and stalks toward me, the circle of Holmes Corps Black parting to allow him out.

"You're supposed to be here to help," he says tersely. "Not to *blaspheme*."

Then the enormous statue speaks. Thephal's jaws grind open, but the voice issues from all the cracks in the statue simultaneously: an echoing, thready, breathy sound more like wind sighing over rocks than humanoid speech. But there *are* words, definite and distinct.

"*Let the god-touched through.*"

The voice surprises us all. This time everyone, not just Jeong$_2$, falls to their knees on the hard floor. Only the three of us are left standing, goggling at each other.

"I don't know which of us counts as 'god-touched,' so let's all three of us approach the nice lady," I suggest to my friends.

Nadia nods and takes my hand. I touch Milly's fingers with my other hand; she gets the hint and curls her big hand around mine.

"I see it," Milly whispers. "Frothing in a, a giant goddess-shaped container. The magic is so bright it hurts my eyes."

When she "sees" magic, she really does have eyes, even if they're not visible to the rest of us. I murmur, "You don't have to look right at it."

We step closer to the possessed statue of Thephal. I

crane my neck up at its "face," if only because it's easier for me to address something with facial features.

"You're what the woman on the spider wants to get at," I say. "To destroy. Is that right?"

"*Bloated Belly can never destroy me,*" comes the reply, carried on the wind from the cracks. The eyes in the dark fissures are rolling wildly when they aren't staring me down.

"It sure seems to be trying. And destroying everything else in the process."

"*As long as my people believe in Fath the Giver,*" answers the statue, "*they will prevail.*"

"But 'Fath the Giver' is a fraud," I say. "Isn't it?"

The corps magicians prostrated around us let us a collective mutter of anger. None of them dare to interrupt this conversation with their deity, however.

The statue startles me by chuckling—or that's how I interpret the sudden, piping notes that issue from it, as if from an organ. "*Am I a fraud if I wear more than one name? Your friend may know me as Breath of the Abyss, but that is one of many names. None adequately describe my power.*"

"It *is* true," Nadia mumbles. "Once a windbag, always a windbag..."

"I don't care what you call yourself," I tell the cracked statue. "You're a fraud because you pretend you're the source of all magic in this world. People believe you 'gave' them all the different types of magic, and you encourage that belief. But for most of it, you're only a kind of activator, aren't you? The magic is *in* them already—in us otherworlders too. The five types come from the five elements—the only type you can truly take credit for is wind. The 'know-it-alls.'"

Jeong$_2$ glances up at me from the floor. "Stop this, you—you idiot! Fath will strike you down for this talk. Maybe the rest of us too."

"Let it, then," I say, with more bravery than I feel. "Breath of the Abyss... if you champion learning and knowledge and growth, all those worthy Notions, then you're holding yourself to those ideals too. Can you justify hitting me with a lightning bolt for speaking the truth?"

"*No,*" the statue answers. "*I could counter you with the ultimate truth—burst these marble bonds and annihilate you with my divine presence, which no mortal can look on without perishing. But that would have the unfortunate side effect of annihilating my faithful followers as well. Tell me, god-touched, do you understand the nature of your own magic?*"

"I'm a creep," I say. "I'm the weirdo who got touched by the Hand That Never Closes, so it makes total sense—quintessence is behind both healing and harming magic. The Hand dances on that line between life and death." I indicate Milly at my side. "Milly's blocking magic is affiliated with earth; that's also why she can hear and communicate with the spiders, because they're of that element. Nadia and the other mindfuckers—that must be water magic. She told me the Bloody Swarm loves to fuck with people's heads, and Shaughnessy's tidal rod came from a water Port world.

"That leaves... heartburners associated with fire. The clue's right in the nickname. And you're the master of wind Ports. And time, maybe, since your people can generate magic powerful enough to glimpse into the past or future. Again, the 'know-it-all' nickname makes it pretty clear to me that that type of magic is your domain—but the other elements originate elsewhere."

Milly touches my shoulder. "Hey. I'm sure it's satisfying to diss a god to its face... but what are we accomplishing here?"

"The point is," I say, "that this *isn't* a god. No more than the Hand That Never Closes is. Or Bloated Belly, Fifty

Furred Limbs. They're—beings of some sort, and obviously they have powers and knowledge beyond our imagining. But they don't deserve to be worshiped just for that."

"Some people would have a hard time making the distinction," Nadia points out.

"Well, part of it's—semantics!" I say, starting to get exasperated. "Call them gods or not, but don't worship them. In the end, they're petty little fuckers. Breath of the Abyss! Why did Bloated Belly enter this world?"

"*To unseat me,*" the statue says with refreshing honesty. "*Every world I rule, every new population of followers I build makes me stronger. Every world another Master takes from me, weakens me. We all of us have been engaged in this game of worlds for aeons, but it is the antithesis of 'petty,' god-touched. Hear me well—if one of the Masters gains supremacy over all others, the multiverse as you know it will cease to exist. Balance MUST be maintained.*"

"But *you* wouldn't refuse that power if it was available to you, would you?" I ask the being in the statue.

"*You do me a disservice, Divya Allard. I seek only to maintain balance. It is the other Masters who are mad for power. Like Bloated Belly. Or the Master dwelling inside you. I venerate only wisdom and learning. Look at the world I have fostered.*"

"This *was* a beautiful world before Bloated Belly wrecked it," Nadia says.

She has a point, and so does Breath of the Abyss. But I'm not inclined to take any of these "Masters" at their word. "So if we help you drive Bloated Belly off your turf—then we're helping restore balance to the multiverse? But what if Bloated Belly is balancing *you* out after you've expanded too far? Is there a scorecard I could look at?"

The statue lets out that piping chuckle again. "*You will have to decide on your own. Whether to ally yourself with beauty and learning, or destruction and ruin. The choice is yours—I will not make it for you.*"

"Incoming," Milly mutters abruptly. "Spider—big one—*incoming!*"

All of the Holmes Corps Black magicians rise to their feet. Jeong$_2$ does too, and he looks sharply at Milly. "She can sense them? With that helmet of hers?"

"Yeah," I say, not taking the time to correct him. "Magic helmet. Are these people rested up enough to withstand another attack?"

"No," says Ropha, the Latina woman who spoke to Jeong$_2$ earlier. "But *you're* here to help—aren't you? What's your power?"

"My big fat mouth," I say. "And I'm all talked out."

I hear it coming now too, feel the vibrations under my feet. Milly's right: a big one. Gonna be bigger than any of the spiders we've seen so far. Beside me, Nadia braces herself. "Maybe I can fool it somehow," she says. "I don't know what I'm capable of—maybe not much—but—"

I turn to her, filled with a sick certainty. "Save your energy. Illusions don't work on this one, if it's gotten this far. You'll need your strength to run. To get to Back Bay and spring that lock so Jeong can get Benazir out. You're the only one with a Compass, you're the only one who can coordinate with him across worlds. Get out now!"

"No freaking way!" Nadia gets right in my face, practically spraying me with spittle. "I'm not leaving you here to die, so *forget it!*"

Stupid fool. How am I going to get her out of here now?

Then an ugly idea hits me and won't let go.

Trying to control myself as my panic rises and a terrible screeching fills my ears, I scream back at Nadia. "I'm not in love with you—give it up already and go! You had it right back on the boat. There's no way I'll ever get over Hannah. We were *engaged*. You think you could ever take her place, because you—"

No, now's not the time to mention Nadia's bravery, her shining eyes, her quick wit and phenomenal sense of adventure, her exceptional body... God's sake!

"—dammit, you let the city councilors *get* her, thanks to your, your laissez-faire style of leadership in your irresponsible little fucking cult! And now you think you deserve to be by my side?"

Nadia Chopin rears back from me. Her features crumple. She looks twice as pale as usual, every freckle standing out on her face like a tiny wound. She stumbles toward the doorway.

"Jesus *Christ,* Allard, what's gotten into you?" Milly roars.

That's when the whole room shakes from two many-branching limbs slamming onto the jagged rim of the hole in the ceiling. Debris rains down on us.

"*Now!*" Ropha screams. "*Give it all you fucking got!*"

All the HCB magicians direct their attention toward the opening in the ceiling. Yelling as they do so, they join their will together into an immense burst of withering magic that makes a visible path upward by displacing the air around it. The gigantic, furry legs curl around the edge of the hole, other legs dangling from them at the joints. A grotesque spider head, sporting huge pincers and dozens of tiny alien eyes, looms through the hole as the air displacement reaches the same spot.

The pincers clack. The head rears back. But it doesn't go away.

The magicians around me sag in defeat and fear. I return my gaze upward to the awful spider face peeking through the breached ceiling. Then it shifts and a much smaller, human face becomes visible above the spider's maw.

"Please give up," the girl calls down to us. A teenager, the same one I remember acting as a lookout when I first went through the Port to Stroyer's Axle. One of the youngest Portwalkers I've met, and most definitely someone who shouldn't have been entrusted with knowledge of the multiverse.

"If you leave this room, it's—it's promised not to kill you," she goes on. "We're only after the statue."

16

The identity of the pregnant woman was one mystery I couldn't solve until the answer simply showed up. But Nadia is right—*who* the girl is doesn't matter. What matters is what's she done, and how we can undo it.

Jeong$_2$ raises his Springfield M1A to the ceiling. I slap its steel barrel away and he looks at me, astounded by my nerve.

"Before you murder her," I growl at him, "give me a shot. That's what I'm here for, right?"

He gives me a stiff nod and lowers the semi. "You *better* make a difference, quick."

I shout upward, "Kid! You can stop this right now!"

"D-does she know you?" Jeong$_2$ asks.

"Not well," I say.

The girl's face is pale and frightened, not the confident face of a conqueror. She's exactly how Tucker and LaPlante$_2$ described: heavily pregnant, as impossible as it seems. She holds one hand over her distended stomach and looks down at me blankly. Then she shouts, "Detective *Allard?* What are you doing here?!"

"Was gonna ask you the same, honey," I call back. "Why don't you climb down from that monster and we can chat? What's your name?"

"Doreen," she says. "And I can't climb down—it won't let me."

"What won't?"

She points down at the spider's face. It's staring at me with animal cunning. I don't imagine it having an intention, a will, unless it's tied in directly with its master, Bloated Belly, Fifty Furred Limbs. Maybe the spiders are all part of a hive mind directed by Bloated Belly. Or maybe…

"Milly, you talked to the spiders back at the Ballroom," I say. "You *convinced* them to do something. Think you could do the same with this one?"

"I can try." She pulls her helmet tighter down onto her head—a nervous habit, as the helmet has nothing to do with communicating with spiders—and lowers her head, muttering under her breath.

Jeong$_2$ whacks my shoulder with the barrel of his rifle. "Hey. Officer Fragonard *talks to spiders*?"

"Shut up and let her concentrate."

"Nah, I don't think so," Jeong$_2$ says, more loudly this time. "If you people can talk to the spiders, that means you're in *league* with them. The spider-woman even knows you by name! So I don't know what you're having Officer Fragonard say to the spider, but she needs to stop right now. Or I shoot her."

When I don't answer him, he shoves the M1A's barrel into my stomach and screams at me, "*Do you hear me?!*"

"That's enough! Drop it!"

He whirls to see Nadia Chopin somehow right behind

him. She holds a big, shiny pistol up to his forehead. She repeats, "Drop it! Drop it now!"

Jeong$_2$ drops the semi, and I immediately snatch it up. Then Nadia disappears into thin air. He blinks at the space where she was, shocked—and now disgusted with himself.

Nadia, the real Nadia, is standing by the doorway. She looks grey in the face from the illusion she created, but she throws me a vicious grin and says, "You're not gonna get rid of me that easily. You absolute bitch."

Above us, the spider cocks its head. One of its freaky limbs unfurls all the way to the shining floor, scattering exhausted creeps who have no defenses left but their own two feet. The legs hanging off it dance and jerk in the air.

"Did it work?" Milly asks me, finished with her trance. "I see *something*, but I don't..."

"Yes. Spider dropped a leg down. Like—" I get it. "A ladder."

"Climb down, Doreen," Milly calls up. "You may not get another chance."

Doreen moans, "Oh shit." But she clambers around the spider's ugly head and shimmies down the extended leg. Her massive belly slows her down and makes her movements awkward, but Doreen manages to get all the way down to the floor, where she collapses, exhausted. Nadia and I rush to her, pulling her up and getting her off her belly. Doreen's auburn hair is sweat-plastered to her face and she's panting.

I open my mouth to pepper her with questions, but the spider screeches then, loud enough to make my ears ring in pain. Its leg rears up, hovering above our heads, ready to smash all our skulls open.

"Keep me with you," Doreen gasps. "Keep me close to

you and you'll be safe. It wants me alive. *Don't let it take me back.* Please!"

Nadia and Milly and I form a tight knot around Doreen, tripping over our own feet as we move backwards with her to help her get out of the questing leg's range.

"Is that spider Bloated Belly itself?" I ask.

"No," Nadia and Doreen answer at the same time.

Doreen gives Nadia a curious, almost hostile look and then clarifies: "I've seen Bloated Belly, Fifty Furred Limbs. Talked to it. It's much bigger. And smarter. You wouldn't be able to plant suggestions in its head."

The spider screeches again, the rage plain in its horrible voice. Its leg swings around, sweeping the floor, and catches three unlucky HCB magicians that hadn't been smart enough to flee once their magic ran out. One is crushed in the embrace between leg joints, jellied organs squirting out of the spider's grip from above and below. The other two scream as they lift off the ground, borne toward the spider's furiously scissoring pincers. I can't watch what happens next.

As if in response, Doreen's belly bulges with movement under the surface. She lets out a miserable cry and clutches her stomach.

I don't see it as the most important question, but Nadia asks anyway: "Whose baby is that? How the fuck did it grow so fast?"

Doreen directs her red-rimmed eyes at her and whispers, "That's no baby."

∻

As we're all gathered so closely around Doreen, none of us can help our instinct to recoil from her—from that writhing belly. Only the memory of her warning to stick close to her keeps me from running to the other side of the room. *What's in there?!*

I'll have to get the story from her later. Right now an enormous spider leg crashes back down into the central chamber, perilously close to the statue of Thephal. Fath, or rather Breath of the Abyss, didn't move an inch to help any of its faithful when they were being attacked. It doesn't move to avoid the leg either. Another of the spider's legs rips the hole in the ceiling wider; more of its gross body becomes visible, including the pale undercarriage.

Thephal's expression seems smug to me now. *Fuck it, let the spider get it.*

Then I think of Tucker and her boat colony. I think of young Roderick Lord, daring to defy LaPlante$_2$'s orders. And Portsmouth$_2$, which may have a survivor or two yet.

"We can't let that thing destroy the statue," I say. "The old windbag may have other worlds to retreat to, but I have a feeling once it's gone, the remaining people of this world are fucked."

Doreen cries out. Her stomach ripples. Whatever's in her belly wants to get out, and soon.

"Milly!" I say. "Can you talk to Bloated Belly itself? Is there any way?"

"No," Doreen says, the word nearly a sob. "Don't do it. It'll poison you, fill you up the way it did with me."

Milly looks distressed. "I—I don't think I can. Bloated Belly isn't *here*. Only its spiders are. I would need to go to where it is."

"That's not an option."

Doreen arches her back and her bulging belly thrusts out. Her fingers form claws as she rakes at our arms. "Oh *fuck*," she moans.

"Friends, I think Bloated Belly will be here real soon," Nadia says, staring at Doreen's stomach with dreadful fascination.

NO. "*Through* her?" I say. "It'll kill her!"

"And the rest of us," Milly says.

I look up at the statue of Thephal. "Fath! Do you have any power at all or are you completely useless?! This is your world, so do something!"

"*What do you wish?*" whistles the voice from the cracks, where eyes peep at us with avaricious interest.

"Help me talk to Bloated Belly itself so I can get it to stop!"

One of the spider legs bashes against the statue. Fragments of marble go flying, and the air rushing out of the cracks grows stronger with more room to escape. Thephal's jaws grind.

"*I will leave this place,*" says Breath of the Abyss. "*My followers were not worthy enough or strong enough to withstand the army of Bloated Belly, Fifty Furred Limbs. Here I have lost the game of worlds, but I can win in another place.*"

"No! Don't up and *leave,* you goddamn bastard!"

"*Kill the vessel for Bloated Belly and you will prevent it from entering this world; only its servants will remain. But you must hurry.*"

Doreen screams, falling back against the floor and convulsing. Her legs open as if by their own will.

"No, I'm not killing this 'vessel,'" I shout at the cracked statue. "There has to be another way!"

"*She will die as Bloated Belly is born here, and it won't be gentle. You'll be doing her a kindness.*" Breath of the Abyss is sounding bored. I notice several eyes in the fissures are closing. The winds emitting from the statue are calming. It *is* leaving.

I have to get to Bloated Belly, Fifty Furred Limbs. And then I realize how.

"Help me get her pants down," I order Nadia as I undo Doreen's belt. The poor girl lets me, barely conscious of what's going on around her. She's thrashing in pain.

"*What?* Divya, we *don't* want Bloated Belly to come into this world!"

But Nadia helps me get Doreen's pants and drawers off. The girl's nether regions are pulsing and expanding like her belly itself, and they're giving off an uncanny glow.

"Somehow Doreen's become a human Port," I say. My heart is racing and I feel delirious, but the insane words I'm speaking are true. "And Ports work both ways."

"Oh my god," Milly says. "We have to—what, go *through* her before it does? But, but *how*?"

"No, you're staying here." I haven't forgotten what she told me in the boat, her dreams about Bloated Belly.

"Allard, you *need* me to be there. I have a connection to Bloated Belly."

"That's exactly why I don't want you anywhere near that thing! You said it wanted to *claim* you, right?"

She huffs. "Stop acting like I have any choice in the matter. This is like when you asked me to come to this world in the first place. You knew I couldn't say no if people's lives were at stake. And you know I have to come with you now. You just want to make yourself feel better by putting up a token resistance."

Argh. "Milly—"

"And don't try to tell me you don't love me or whatever," she interrupts me, with a bitterly ironic smile. "That trick isn't gonna work on me either."

"Fine! Fath, don't you dare peace out until I get my wish granted!" I holler at the statue. "Help me—help Milly and me get through the Port before Bloated Belly gets here first! Help us get through without killing Doreen!"

"*It may be a one-way journey*," answers Breath of the Abyss, sounding further away than before. Few of its eyes are now visible, and the statue only radiates wisps of air. "*But I will grant you this boon.*"

The wind from the statue strengthens, though it changes direction, wrapping around and around Milly Fragonard and me, whirling faster until I can no longer see my own hands in front of me. My stomach lurches as a profound vertigo hits me, knocks me over, or rather it would if I were sure I have a *body*—but I'm not. I've lost all sensation and senses except for vision, as if I've become one of Fath's floating eyeballs.

And I see the world around me looming larger, including Doreen herself, her smooth flesh making itself into an undulating landscape rising on all sides of me. That forbidden Port at her cleft becomes gigantic, whirling rocks and dust tracing a wild circle around it. I drift toward the Port—through it—

Into darkness.

I don't know if I have a mouth anymore, or a voice. But I give it a try. "Milly?!"

My shout echoes off the unseen space. From the way the sound travels, I'd guess I'm in a cavern of incredible dimensions. Alone?

"Allard!"

Never has another human voice sounded so welcome. If I have a voice and a mouth with which to speak it, maybe I have the rest of my body back too. I experiment with stepping forward in the dark. The Springfield M1A bumps against my stomach; I forgot it was slung around me. Not that it'll do any good here…

I fumble my way toward Milly. She reaches me first and takes my hand. Of course; this darkness won't make much of a difference to her.

"Where are we?" she asks.

"If I had to guess... the home world or plane of Bloated Belly," I reply. "But what that means, I'm not sure."

I blink as something disrupts the absolute darkness: a cube. A floating cube, glowing silvery-white, bobbing through the dark and growing larger, which might mean that it's getting closer. From somewhere in the cube's direction, a harsh voice speaks.

"*The Prime of All Earth. And* you *don't belong here.*"

The sound is like gravel rolling down a hill, like boulders sliding against each other. I face the cube. "Bloated Belly, I presume?"

"*Quintessence-filthy girl. You stain the purity of this place. How dare you come here?*" The cube surges forward and grows brighter. It's a couple of feet long on each side. I catch a few small reflections of the light now, below the cube. Eyes? Maybe I don't want to look.

No. I definitely don't. I remember now—both the Hand That Never Closes and Breath of the Abyss warned me that looking at them in their full forms would destroy me. I'll have to assume the same holds true for Bloated Belly, Fifty Furred Limbs.

"Don't look too closely at it," I mutter in Milly's direction.

"*Ah, but this one with you is more pleasing to me. My own kind. Isn't that right, eyeless one?*"

"Oh god," Milly says in a throaty voice. "Whatever you are, we've got nothing in common."

Chittering resonates in the darkness. The cube dims and then brightens again. "*Millicent Fragonard. Your tide answers to me. You belong to me. Have you not seen that this is so, in dreams?"*

Milly doesn't answer.

"You have the potential to see so much further, eyeless one. Awaken yourself to me and I will show you all that you can become. Come, Millicent, and touch the cube."

"*No!*" Milly barks at the unseen creature.

The negotiation is not going well. I step in. "Listen—ugh—Bloated Belly. We came here to stop you from going through the..." I turn, realizing I can't see the Port we somehow entered through. "Breath of the Abyss told us it'd be extremely bad if any one of you five... Port masters became dominant. End-of-the-multiverse bad. You need to stay out of its world to maintain balance."

"*Balance?*" The voice of Bloated Belly turns to pebbles skittering one by one over glass. "*Filth of the Hand, you understand nothing. I make my move to restore balance. Breath of the Abyss has grown too strong, with believers in too many worlds. I must counteract its spread.*"

"Funny, that's what Breath of the Abyss said about *you*. Is that what you all say about each other?"

"*I am the guardian of generations across every universe. I am the mother of mothers and the father of fathers, the master and the architect of every birth that happens in every world. I am the seed and the egg. I am your parents copulating in Bengaluru. I have no interest in seeing generations end as the stars collapse.*"

The creature shifts in the darkness and the cube shifts with it. I'm getting the idea that the cube occupies a fixed position above it, perhaps above its head, but again I don't want to look more closely.

"You could all be liars as far as I know," I say. "Unless you're willing to share the tally sheet with me. How many worlds does Breath of the Abyss dominate right now, and how many do you dominate?"

"*A meaningless question. I cannot explain the reckoning to you. You are like an ant trying to learn calculus. Begone to whence you came and let me speak to Millicent Fragonard alone.*"

I'm not sure I even can go back, but I'm not going to leave Milly here. "Leave Earth-two alone," I say, "and let Doreen return to normal. You already caused Breath of the Abyss to vacate the world, and killed millions of its believers… shouldn't that count as a victory?"

"*I am a god, quintessence filth! I cannot be bargained with, I cannot be pleaded with, and I cannot be defeated. There is only one price I will consider, and I will name it, not you.*" The cube glows brighter until I have to look away. "*Millicent! Touch the cube and awaken the full potential of your tide. Do this and I will remain in the Prime of All Earth. I will not enter the ruined world.*"

Something is stirring in my mind. I recognize the muttering of the Hand, though I can't make it out. *Quiet*, I hiss back.

"Allard, this is why I'm here," Milly says dreamily. "I understand now. With a touch, I can save the survivors we met."

"No, you can't," I say. "It's never just a touch. This thing wants to *own* you and whatever power you have."

She scoffs. "How much of a dumbbell do you think I am? I *know*. It'll use me until I'm empty. But can I put my own stunted life over everyone else's?"

"Yes, you can and you will. I won't let you near that fucking thing."

"You don't get to decide."

"The hell I don't!" I grope for her hand in the dark.

"Come on, we're going to find the exit. Bloated Belly's probably lying anyway."

"*I am not.*"

"Stop it, Allard!" Milly snaps, and she slaps my hand away. "I get to make one last meaningful decision in my life after all the things I had no choice over. Don't you dare try to take my choice away now, or I swear—"

Divya. The Hand's thick voice is clearer now in my mind, surging forward. *Surrender yourself to me now. You have brought me this far—you have brought me into the very lair of my enemy. Let me strike at it.*

"No, I'm sure you're a liar too," I say, angrily and aloud.

"Now you're calling *me* a liar?" Milly says in outrage. "How can you—"

The Hand speaks again in my head. *You cannot fight a god but with a god. Do it or your friend's life is forfeit. You can see it plainly.*

"*Who are you talking to?*" Bloated Belly growls, its voice like a cave-in thudding into my skull. "*Filth of the Hand, have you let your master into this place?!*" For the first time, I can detect an unsteady note in the creature's blunt and bullying tone. "*I have tolerated you too long!*"

Let go. Do it now!

The glowing cube moves forward, accompanied by the noise of many rustling, stamping limbs—more than fifty, surely. I stumble backwards and I sense Milly moving too. Toward the cube.

I close my eyes and surrender to the presence of the Hand, the same way I did in the Doxe's palace in Avariccia. My mind yields to the quintessence master's mind, my mouth to its mouth. When I speak next, it's in the guttural tone of the Hand That Never Closes.

"You will remain here," it says through me, to the unseen

Bloated Belly. "You will send these two women back to the library and you will cleanse the girl of your foul earth."

That voice stops both Milly and Bloated Belly in their tracks.

"*Arrogant corpse!*" roars Bloated Belly, Fifty Furred Limbs. "*Grasping ghoul! I should have known you lurked inside your filthy servant! I will do none of what you say!*"

"You will do all of it," says the Hand through me, "or I will release myself through this vessel and bury you in your cavern forever. You know as soon as I step through, this plane will be tainted beyond repair."

Release itself? I think, panicked, in whatever corner of my head my own mind has been shoved into. And then I realize —yes, why *couldn't* it happen? If Bloated Belly could use Doreen's body as a Port to travel through, couldn't the Hand do the same with my own body?

And then, of course, that'll be the end of *me*...

"*She has walked in the Prime of All Quintessence?*" Bloated Belly says—or rather shrieks, like a grindstone against metal. "*She is a gate?!*"

"Yes, and I will open her unless you do all that I have commanded, now," the Hand orders.

"*You will regret this. I will send all of my beasts and all of my tendrils questing toward your worlds, Hand. I will consume your very being and become the master of life AND death. You will see! You will see!*"

"NOW, eater of dirt." I feel my lips curling into a grim smile.

Bloated Belly lets out a terrible thundering cry, as if giving voice to tectonic plates sliding over each other. Small rocks strike me, and dust clouds my vision of the cube. It flies into my mouth, which the Hand doesn't have the good sense to keep shut, and I choke on the grit. Stones are battering me from all sides—I get to feel the pain but not have the control to do anything about it. I hear Milly crying out.

Then I'm blind and turning in the darkness, rotating, flying, and my body itself feels as hard as stone, devoid of human sensation. I'm like an asteroid, a dead hunk of rock hurtling through space.

My body, or whatever it's become, shudders as it strikes a surface. Then my pain sensors awaken, and with them, the rest of me. I open my eyes to a magnificent wall hanging of Fath the Giver surrounded by prophets and peasants and kings, all performing the Hundred Deeds that would make way for the gift of magic. The magnificence of the wall hanging, however, is marred by large shreds torn away, leaving many Deeds missing.

I tear my gaze away and sit up in a hurry. The reading room is littered with the bodies of magicians who failed to escape the spider's wrath, including Ropha. The statue of Thephal is gone, destroyed by the huge spider legs, which are currently nowhere to be seen.

Milly is splayed on the floor nearby, her helmet dented and smashed, but she's breathing. The girl Doreen is with us too, patting her flattened stomach in wonder, tears streaking through the grime on her face. She hasn't thought to pull her pants up yet.

Completing our disheveled knot on the library floor, Nadia lies facedown—her body a pulpy, broken mess. Big pieces of marble from the fallen statue surround her.

17

I crawl over to Nadia Chopin's shattered body. I'm breathing in shallow, horrified gasps. From the way she's positioned, she was shielding Doreen from the falling statue or the onslaught of the spider's monstrous limbs, or both.

I put my bloody fingers on her neck. She's alive, but her breath is faint.

Help me, I implore the Hand That Never Closes. But it's gone. It's accomplished its goal, back in the Prime of All Earth, I'm sure to some mysterious end that serves it better than me. Now it's relinquished my body and silenced its own voice.

"Oh no," Milly wheezes nearby. "Allard—is Nadia okay? I don't—I can't sense her magic anymore."

"She'll be fine," I say. I'm crying into Nadia's dark-blonde hair, now streaked with red. I have to pull it together.

Place both hands on your patient, Elthaba said. Or maybe it was Elliott. *Focus your intention. What you are sharing is not just magic, but your heart. There is no healing that can be done without love.*

I don't even have the energy to stand up, much less to properly focus on the monumental task ahead of me. But I put my palms down on the ruin of Nadia's shoulders and I narrow my vision to a small slice of the distressing sight of her. I force myself to breathe deeper, to relax my own body into a meditation.

After a time, my hands glow. But they're not glowing enough.

It's happening again. I'm going to let her die. Like I let Arreth die.

No!

My breathing is erratic now. Have to slow it down. Have to do it for her.

I'm hurting all over from our violent journey back through the Port of Doreen. I'm full of despair that no heart-burner instilled in me. I'm sick with worry for people in two different worlds. But all of that slowly, gently sinks down into the hidden core of me as I regulate my breathing and I look at Nadia. I look at her with love.

I remember her marching down the street with the 3Peter protesters. I remember her in her office, forcing me to recognize that the Relic I'd brought to her was a fingernail of the Hand itself. *Not all gods exist, but that doesn't mean that some don't.* I remember her kissing me across the table in Stroyer's Axle.

That light that you're radiating, Divya—I want it inside me, too.

She believed I had light in me long before my hands ever started to glow. The least I can do now is share it with her.

The light in my hands intensifies. I lean forward and kiss Nadia's bloodied lips.

Then she bucks under my palms. I tilt my head back, out of the way, as she lets out a long, loud scream.

"Holy crap," Milly says, nearby, as Doreen adds, "*Is she dying?*"

So yeah, the noise has kind of ruined the air of desperate romance and tragedy. But Nadia screaming means that the healing is *working*.

"Help me hold her in place!" I say to the other two women, not daring to move my hands or even swivel my head. I won't let Nadia out of my sight until this is over.

Doreen leans on Nadia's feet. Bareheaded Milly feels around until she's positioned herself over Nadia's thrashing torso and can hold her arms down. I let healing flow from me, from reserves I never knew existed, into Nadia's body, and she screams and screams as her tissue mends itself and her terrible wounds knit and close.

By the time it's done, and Nadia's screaming has died down to whimpers and groans, I feel like I've run a marathon. Or pushed a boulder up a mountain. The glow in my hands is now a faint radiance. Nadia twitches as her body continues to repair itself. I slouch, my head dropping halfway to my knees, and Milly brings a canteen of water to my lips. I drink. She gets some water down Nadia's throat too.

"We can give you a place to rest."

I look up and see Jeong$_2$ standing over us. He looks weary and contrite. A couple of the surviving HCB magicians file into the chamber as well.

"Thanks, but no thanks," I say. "We've got places to be. Where's the giant spider?"

"Gone underground," Jeong$_2$ says. "It seemed to lose its motivation. I guess it did what it came here to do." He glances at the spot where the statue of Thephal once stood. Only the feet are intact.

"We could use a ride to the FBI field office in Back Bay," I suggest.

He looks doubtfully at Nadia, who is lying down and not moving much anymore. "If you say so." Then his eye lands on Doreen. Her pallor is back to normal and she looks like a healthy young woman of nineteen or twenty, not the type to ride a monstrous spider or give birth to a world-ending god. "How did she... where is her baby?"

"You missed that part," Milly says. "She was gonna give birth to the leader of the spiders, but we put a stop to that."

"Still awfully tingly down there though," Doreen says, her cheeks reddening.

Jeong$_2$ stares at her, then turns back to me. "I don't understand... any of this. I mean, the big spider's gone, so yay for that, but—I need time to process everything that's happened. Tell me one thing—" He pauses. "Is Fath coming back?"

I frown. "I don't know. I wouldn't count on it."

"Word got out, from some of the Holmes Corps Black folks who ran away... word spread that Fath is gone. And now all the Corps magic protecting the city is faltering. People are losing their faith. I don't know what I can tell them to get it back."

"Tell them the magic comes from themselves," I say. "Fath didn't give them anything. Their belief in their own collective power is what's been keeping them going all this time."

Jeong$_2$ regards me coldly. "It's a little *soon* to ask people to throw away their lifelong religion. Come on; if you want that ride, you'll have to hoist her up. I'd offer to take her—or all of you—to the hospital, but Holmes Corps White is faltering like all the rest."

"We need to get one last thing done," I assure him, "and then we're going home."

And I *am* determined to get the three of us home—and Doreen too—even if we have to hitchhike all the way back up to Portsmouth$_2$. I'm holding on to the hope that, like Doreen's former ride, all the other spiders have lost their appetite too now that Bloated Belly isn't coming.

I crouch by Nadia and ask her, softly, "How are you doing?"

She lets out a long groan. But then her green eyes focus on me. "You did it," she whispers.

"You ready for a car ride?"

"No. Not at all."

"Okay, then let's go," I say. The fact that she's conscious and capable of speech is all that I need. She'll have to be ready.

Milly and Doreen and I help Nadia to her feet, but we find she can't walk even with our assistance. So we—okay, mostly Milly—heft her up and carry her out out of the library, following Jeong$_2$, who is hurrying ahead but also making frequent stops to communicate with someone on his phone. Though being womanhandled over a considerable distance can't be too much fun for her, Nadia gets a big, silly grin on her face.

"Divya," she says. "You kissed me, right? I didn't dream that?"

"Yep."

"Can we do that again?"

Oh boy. I remember the "healing high" I myself experienced back at the boat colony after Elthaba and Elliott were done with me. "Let's hold that thought for now."

"How did you make it back out of Doreen's va—"

"Heeey," I interrupt her loudly, "look, we're almost to Jeong-two's car. Jeong-two, can you open the back door please?"

He nods and scrambles to open the backseat for us. "You said 'back door,'" Nadia giggles as we bundle her in.

Blushing Doreen and stalwart Milly take either side of Nadia, propping her up in the middle of the backseat, and I circle around to take the front passenger. Jeong$_2$ gives me side-eye as he gets behind the wheel. I shrug at him and say, "I take it your Longfellows didn't see this all coming."

"If they did, they didn't share it with me," he says and guns the engine. "Where to?"

I give him the address. The street name trips up the GPS on his phone; dimensional differences, apparently. He calls up the map. We fumble back and forth with identifying local landmarks until we nail down approximately where the FBI Field Office should be in this world. Then we hit the road.

Almost immediately, Nadia says, "Hey. My arm's pulsing. Ethan."

Milly puts her fingers to the Compass on Nadia's wrist. "Give me a minute to translate. The pattern's repeating."

"Translate?" I say, confused.

"The Morse code," Milly answers. "Like I did on the boat, the last time he got in touch. Oh... you were passed out then."

Ah. That would be what Ethan and Milly discussed on the phone back at the Lord house, rather than a flirtatious chat. Oh well—I can still ship them in my mind. "When did you learn Morse code?"

"When she was a kid, she wanted to be a signalwoman

for the Navy," Nadia answers me. "Shhhh, let her interpret it."

Milly decodes the short and long pauses. "Ethan wants to know where we are."

"Tell him we'll be there soon," I say. "Well, tell him the minutes—how many, Jeong-two?"

"Five," Jeong$_2$ says. "Why do you keep calling me 'two' and isn't Ethan the guy you confused me for? He's at the FBI office now?"

"Sort of."

"Sort of?!"

Now's not the time to educate Jeong$_2$ about parallel worlds. I redirect the conversation. "Doreen—can you tell us how you came to ruin this world, in five minutes or less?"

"Allard," Milly says.

Doreen waves her objection away. "It's okay. I deserve it. Listen, Nadia, I know you told us to always use the buddy system. I should have done that when I found a new earth Port. But I couldn't resist going in by myself. I felt drawn to it."

"Must be your type of tide," Nadia mumbles. "Go on."

"Wait, where was this Port?" I cut in.

"In Portsmouth," Doreen says, giving me a rare defiant look. "That's all I want to say for now—I don't want to endanger anyone else. Anyway... it was a big, dark cavern. I could hardly see anything and I was scared. This voice coming from a glowing cube beckoned me closer. It told me to touch the cube and everything would be all right. So I did."

"Never touch the cube," Nadia mutters.

Doreen looks down at her before continuing. "The top of it *opened* and... filled me up. With this terrible, earthy stuff. I felt my stomach growing, rounding out, and it felt like—well—spiders were squirming around inside me. The voice cut through my screaming and said if I wanted to be rid of it, I would need to perform a simple task. I would need to deliver a box to Earth. Simple. I was told not to look inside."

"Hmm," I say. "Deliver the box... you mean the glowing cube?"

"The box had formed inside the cube, somehow. A cardboard box. I lifted it out. It was heavy. Even though I agreed to do the delivery, I feared what was in the box. But I took it back with me. To our world. Then it started to shake, on its own."

In *our* world. "Did you look inside it?"

"Not then. But I could guess it was bad news. I had an idea I could *keep* delivering the box, straight on to a different world. I knew there was another Port, right nearby... the Port to this world. I snuck into the Athenaeum and opened the Port and brought the box here. I wasn't even thinking about the consequences of disobeying the voice. I... just couldn't stand being responsible for something bad happening in my own world."

"So you made it *my* world's problem instead," $Jeong_2$ says bitterly. "I should strangle you for that."

But he refrains from stopping the car and wrapping his hands around the girl's neck. I ask, "What happened when you brought the box here?"

"Something was thumping around inside," Doreen says. "I was in the Athenaeum in this world's Portsmouth. I thought—maybe if I opened a window and flung the box out, the drop would kill whatever was inside. So I did that. I looked out the window and saw the box had broken open in

Market Square. Dirt was spilled everywhere. But the dirt was moving. Forming into shapes."

"Spider shapes," Milly guesses.

"Y-yeah. I ran down to the square, with my big belly jiggling. I knew I'd made a terrible mistake. By the time I got there, the spiders had gotten bigger, much bigger, and people nearby were noticing. I ran from the spiders and the people. Then the voice from the darkness spoke in my head."

She pauses, wiping tears from her eyes. "It said I had... displeased it. Failed it. But it would give me one more chance—all I had to do was go down to the library in Boston and knock down a statue. It said it would provide me with a ride. And then the spider found me, the biggest spider of them all, and I was too afraid to disobey. I..." She looks down at where her unnatural pregnancy used to be. "I wanted the things, the *crawling things* inside me to be gone. I knew the voice was probably lying and it would kill me in the end anyway, but I held on to the slim chance it wouldn't."

I look back at her. Her shoulders shake with crying. "It's... okay," I say, though I don't know if it is. I don't know at all. "It's okay."

"You Fath-damned twit," Jeong$_2$ says, hunching over the wheel. "You never asked what the statue was, exactly? You never wondered?"

"That's enough," I say. "Leave her alone."

Jeong$_2$ slams on the brakes. "Get out of the car. All of you. Get out of the fucking car."

"Ethan, please," I say, not realizing my slip-up until it's out of my mouth.

"*My name's not Ethan!*" he screams at me. "Now I want *all of you bitches out of my car NOW* or I'll drive us right into the fucking Charles! I swear to Fath!"

I jump out and hurry to the back to help Doreen and Milly with the Nadia extraction. Doreen is openly weeping, having a hard time holding onto Nadia, so I relieve her and we get our dazed friend a safe distance from the car. Then I turn back and look at the man behind the wheel.

"I'm sorry," I say.

His face is still red, but he sounds calmer as he barks, "You're almost there anyway! You'll figure it out!" $Jeong_2$ spins the car around on the deserted road, back toward the downtown. Then he's gone altogether.

Doreen sits on the curb and puts her head in her crossed arms, distraught. I look at Nadia, who's leaning on Milly; she blinks at me and casts her eyes downward, clearly sharing in the blame for what Doreen did. I sigh and walk over to Doreen. I crouch down next to her and give her shoulder a gentle but awkward pat.

"Doreen," I say. "You fucked up. I won't try to deny that. You should never have gone through the earth Port without knowing what was on the other side, should never have touched that glowing cube. But... you could have destroyed our own world with that box. You didn't. Doreen, you *saved our world*."

Her sobbing eases. She peeks up at me above her crossed arms. "You... think so?"

"Yeah," Milly speaks up. "I think so too." Her words have a rote quality, but they appear to affect Doreen. I boost the signal by offering her my hand.

"Come on," I say. "We've all done good things and shitty things. What's important is that the good outweighs the shitty. We have a friend in trouble who needs our help—will you help us?"

She nods, sniffling, and takes my hand. I bring her to her feet. And the four of us muddle our way to the spot where the FBI field office is. Then we stop and stare.

The building has been leveled. One of the few absolute structural casualties I've seen so far in the City of Notions.

"Oh, *shit*," Nadia exclaims.

"No, it's okay," I say. "We're going to the basement."

18

We step among the wreckage of the field office building until we find the stairwell to the basement. It only takes a few minutes to clear enough junk away to access the stairs.

"I'll lead the way," I say. "Nadia, stay close by me. Doreen, can you take Milly's hand, please?"

The girl glances up at Milly, who's holding her battered helmet under one arm—the damage it sustained while we were leaving the Prime of All Earth has made it unusable. To her credit, Doreen hasn't flinched once at the sight of Milly's eyeless face. "I gotcha," Doreen says, and links her hand with Milly's.

I shine a light down the dark stairs as we head to the basement, steering around wreckage. It occurs to me that if the FBI_2 knew enough about dimension-entangled locks to set them up with the FBI of my world, then the two departments must been in contact with each other. Perhaps the FBI_2 had been planning on exploring Ports too, as soon as they could find one, and it had only been bad luck that they hadn't discovered the Port in the $Athenaeum_2$.

"There are four locks," Nadia says, though I see no change in the darkness beyond the narrow range of my light. "Which one is it?"

"I'll ask Ethan," Milly says. Doreen leads her to Nadia and she puts her fingers on Nadia's wrist, manipulating the Compass to communicate via Morse code. A short time later, Milly speaks up: "Fourth one. Last one."

Nadia walks down the hall, counting off the first three locks. Those cells must house Marsters and her clones in the other world. Then she stops at the fourth.

"Arrange a countdown with Ethan," I order Milly.

"Okay," she says a minute later. "He's ready—standing by. I'm going to do a ten-count. Strike it on zero. Ready?"

I pick up a heavy chunk of concrete.

Milly confirms with Ethan about the count, then says, "OK, ten, nine..."

At "zero," I bring the concrete chunk down hard on the lock. It makes a louder noise than I expect, then the lock vibrates, faster and faster. This must be the "resonance" Nadia anticipated—Ethan must have struck his half at the same instant.

Then the half of the lock in this world flies off and lands at Nadia's feet. A whoosh of air blasts from the fallen lock; we all step back, then we realize that the air isn't exactly air —it's a phantom wind circling around where the lock was, which is now a small, bright hole. I see a black shoe move briefly past the hole on the other side, and instinctively I know it belongs to Ethan Jeong.

"It's a Port," I say. "It's, like, a mini-Port, and now it's open."

A gunshot rings. We all duck, then realize it came from the other side of the Port.

Nadia grunts and holds up her wrist. "I'm getting pulses. Rapid-fire. Same pattern over and over."

Milly feels the device under Nadia's skin. "Three dots, three dashes, three dots. SOS. Ethan's in trouble."

"It's an air Port, like the one we crossed to get here," Nadia says. "Maybe I can expand it. Back up."

She unslings her bag and gets out the plastic baggie of feathers. She traces a rapid, crescent-shaped path on the floor, muttering in the breathy language and flinging feathers toward the little Port on the floor. Slowly it expands.

"Can she go faster?" Doreen asks.

"Quiet," I speak up, "don't rush her."

But Nadia does seem to be moving faster anyway. Soon the Port is big enough to admit a view of an empty room with an overturned chair. I jump through.

The buzzing between worlds is brief but intense. A quick, nearly subconscious image of a hundred staring eyes, eyes that belong to Breath of the Abyss, burns into my mind. Then I stagger as I land in the small, boxy room.

It's not Benazir's cell proper—it's an interview room connected to the cell via glass wall. People can communicate with the prisoner through glass and a microphone system while she stays behind her biplanar lock. Probably the same setup in the other cells too.

The door in the glass wall is unlocked and open, the Port on this side radiating from the discarded lock like on the other side. Benazir isn't in the cell. An operating table is. It's shoved into the corner of the room. Next to it, against the far wall amid an impressionistic haze of blood, slumps a man dressed in surgeon's scrubs. A bullet has obliterated one of his eyes and a generous helping of tissue and bone around the socket. Near his outstretched hand lies a Colt M1911 he won't be needing anymore.

I enter the cell long enough to seize the pistol and then head toward the interview room's other door, leading to the hallway. Nadia stumbles into this world, right next to me. She gawks at the scene in Benazir's cell, but I snap my fingers. "Don't look in there. Hallway. Follow me."

"What happened here," she hisses under her breath, not so much a question as a gut reaction.

Special Agent Ethan Jeong is limping a few yards away under the weight of my doppelganger. Benazir Allard's arm is draped heavily over his shoulders and he has his arm around her waist. Her feet are dragging. They're headed in the opposite direction from the stairwell. All I see at that end of the hall is a closed door with a red security light.

"Ethan!" I shout.

He turns, looking shocked, as Nadia and I run toward him. "How in the hell...?"

Nadia takes the other side of Benazir to lend her muscle to the load. Benazir's eyelids are fluttering, and drool is leaking from her mouth. Maybe the late surgeon drugged her as prep for the live dissection.

"We stretched the lock into a Port," I say. As I point back where I came from, Doreen and Milly pop their heads out of the doorway.

"Good God," Jeong says, "let's go *back* that way. I fucked up. Ivanov is gonna be here any second."

I shake my head. "You don't want to go to that world. Too dangerous."

"It can't be worse than *here*! Oh, shit!"

This last interjection is caused by the sight of a man striding down the hallway. The man's face is pale and sickly-looking under the fluorescents, and his long hair rests on his shoulders limply. ASAC Mark Ivanov carries no weapon I can see, but that makes me even more concerned. Behind him, a bald, brown-skinned man emerges from the stairwell. I remember him too—that's Agent Harriman, Jeong's ally in this office. Perhaps not an ally anymore...

Ivanov wears an easy, triumphant smile as he calls out, "Oh, excuse me! Please don't leave. A procedure is on the schedule for our patient, and I'm afraid it can't be delayed any longer."

"I took pictures of what you did to the others," Jeong says. "I already sent them to a dozen media outlets. You and your whole Frankenstein operation here are finished, Ivanov. We're leaving with this 'patient' now—consider her time served."

Good move, Ethan. Except ASAC Ivanov doesn't look worried at all. "You think I was acting without the full knowledge and approval of the SAC?" he says. "Agent Jeong, you're even more naive than your boyish good looks would lead me to believe."

I catch a look Harriman is directing to Jeong behind Ivanov's back. It says *Sorry.* It says *There's nothing I can do.*

"And thank you, by the way," Ivanov goes on, "for bringing the source material for the clone to me. As you've already seen, the procedures on the Marsters clones did not yield the desired data regarding effects on the source, since she ended her own life prematurely." He sweeps a casual hand toward the outer doors to the three other cells; all three doors are open. "Another chance to observe the interrelated physiologies of clone and source, this time using Benazir and Divya Allard, would be *priceless.*"

I can't help it. I have to look. I walk toward Ivanov until I can get a look in the nearest cell. It's locked, though it no longer needs to be: Kat Marsters, former supervisory special agent of the Portsmouth resident agency, hangs from the ceiling, her features purple and distended.

"It was the screaming, I think," Ivanov says to me softly. "These cells have a regrettable lack of sound-proofing. The sound of her own voice screaming in agony as her first clone underwent the procedure—I fear it may have driven SSA Marsters mad."

He gives me a sly smile. "We'll account for that next time, by fitting you with a pair of noise-canceling headphones as we work on Benazir. If you suffer any ill effects regardless, we'll know there must be some deep link between source and clone, which itself would make for a fascinating field of research."

"You're not going to do any of that," I say.

Ivanov's expression falters. "Oh? And why not? Surely you aren't considering shooting me with that Colt? I guarantee Agent Harriman is a faster shot than you."

"I don't need to shoot you," I reply. "Haven't you wondered how my lady friends and I got in here in the first place? Right now there's an open Port in the middle of your facility. Connecting to a world *destroyed by giant spiders.* Guess what contaminants could be drifting into this place even as we speak?"

The ASAC's mouth drops open.

"I take it you don't have your SAC's approval for *that*?" I say, smiling nastily. "Too bad only my friends and I know how to close that Port."

I sure am glad I remembered my last conversation with this motherfucker, right before he had me arrested and tried to frame me for the murders Benazir committed. Ivanov was obsessed with the potential "contaminants" that my doppelgänger and I could have brought over from Graham's World. As I hoped, the thought of a whole Port's worth of contamination right in the middle of his supposedly secure facility is driving him crazy.

"I'll *make* you close it!" he snaps, losing the fey edge to his tone. "I'll arrest you all and pry the information from your brains while you scream for death!"

"By which time the SAC will know all about the Port," says Agent Harriman.

Ivanov glares at him. Unfazed, Harriman goes on: "Wouldn't you rather the Port be closed by the time the SAC finds out about it? I mean, it's up to you. But I've got him on speed dial, and something like an unauthorized gateway to another universe ought to be reported to the chief right away. I'd be happy to do it."

"You shiny-pated snake," Ivanov growls. "You won't steal my position that way. The SAC hates a snitch."

"Sure about that?" Harriman says.

The long-haired ASAC stalks over to the entrance to Benazir's cell and flinches at the sight of the interview room. He looks from Harriman to Jeong, who's smiling for the first time since I arrived.

"Your move," Jeong says.

ASAC Ivanov makes a fist. Squeezes it. Then opens his palm. He's glumly regarding his empty hand as Milly switches places with Nadia to help Ethan drag limp Benazir to the security door at the end of the hall. Ethan swipes it open with a keycard. Doreen follows them out the door. Harriman keeps a watchful eye on Ivanov as Nadia and I reenter the interview room and she closes the Port.

I give Harriman a wave of gratitude as Nadia and I follow our friends' path to the exit. I have a feeling he'll be the new ASAC after all, once their boss finds out Ivanov was forced to let us all escape to cover his own ass.

I take Nadia's hand as we walk outside to a world blessedly free of mutant arachnids—but perhaps not free of magic, not anymore. Time will tell.

"Let's go home," I say. "We've got more promises to keep."

"Too many," Nadia says.

END OF BOOK 3

COMING FALL 2019

City of Songs
The Shadow Over Portsmouth Book 4

DRAMATIS PERSONAE

EARTH (Master of Ports: Unknown, if any)

Portsmouth, New Hampshire: ***Unaffiliated***
    Divya Allard — former Portsmouth police officer; mentally unstable
    Hannah Ryder — deceased; fiancee to Divya Allard, allegedly killed by Councilor Grace Stone
    Benazir Allard — clone of Divya Allard and serial murderer; prisoner at FBI Boston Field Office
    Kathryn Bergman — therapist to Divya Allard
    Scott Shaughnessy — deceased; former city councilor and owner of Round Island property, killed by Soldier Lord Chaum in Avariccia
    Ilana Stein — deceased; former home aide to Scott Shaughnessy, accidentally killed by Divya Allard
    Val Wegman — disappeared; daughter of Councilor Jack Wegman
    Judah Madbury — disappeared; Val Wegman's boyfriend
    Jed Haven — Keeper, Portsmouth Athenaeum

Deah Sloane — Assistant Keeper, Portsmouth Athenaeum

Lieutenant Bishop — a Coast Guardsman

Sherman — a lobsterman

Vera Tsoukalas — Graham Tsoukalas's mother

Joe Tsoukalas — Graham Tsoukalas's father

Mr. Baldini — head of security at Jacobi Investment Advisors; Divya Allard's former boss

Neria Francoeur — classmate and lover of the late Graham Tsoukalas

Wallace Riggs — classmate and lover of the late Graham Tsoukalas

Rommie McNair — former Portsmouth mayor; keeps geese and sheep

Theo LaPlante — a preacher on Portsmouth public-access television

Derek Ham — painter of bland seascapes

Federal Bureau of Investigation (FBI) Portsmouth Resident Agency

Special Agent Ethan Jeong — acting Portsmouth Supervisory Special Agent

Special Agent Lena Barnes — former partner to Mike McGuinness; blames Divya Allard and Ethan Jeong for McGuinness's death

Special Agent Mike McGuinness — deceased; forced to kill self by Scott Shaughnessy

Special Agent Ximena Ramirez — wounded by Kat Marsters

Portsmouth City Council

Mayor Gantry — mayor and councilor

Grace Stone — assistant mayor and councilor; alleged murderer of Hannah Ryder

Aleksander "Sandy" Grieg — councilor and lawyer

Patricia Gagnon — deceased; former assistant to Councilor Grieg, killed by Divya Allard under mind control from Scott Shaughnessy

A gunman — deceased; employed by Sandy Grieg and killed by Special Agent Ethan Jeong

Christine Figueroa — current assistant to Councilor Grieg; former *Portsmouth Porthole* copy editor

Jack Wegman — councilor and father of Val Wegman

Nancy Cobb — councilor

Hiram Jacobs — councilor

Kevin Waskowski — councilor

Luanne Bourque — councilor

Florence Heath — councilor

Portsmouth Police Department

Chief Henry Akerman — wounded by Benazir Allard

Detective Ben Ulrich — deceased; killed and eaten by Avariccians

Detective Rick McLaren — current detective

Detective Ken Berger — deceased; killed by Benazir Allard

Officer Milly Fragonard — captured and blinded in Avariccia; freed by Divya Allard

Officer Skip Bradley — deceased; killed by Benazir Allard

Officer Burt Daniels — deceased; killed by Benazir Allard

Officer Gary Piotrowski — deceased; killed by Benazir Allard

Officer Mike Prince — suspended, currently under

investigation for murder of Portwalkers Jill Haven and Eddie Barndollar

Officer Leon Gomez — implicated in potential crimes against Portwalkers

Officer Vin Lewis — implicated in potential crimes against Portwalkers

Officer Kate Haring — current officer

Barb Okefor — a lawyer

Portwalkers (Cult within Tenacious Trainers exercise club)

Nadia Chopin — de facto leader of Portwalkers; kissed Divya Allard

Trig — science-oriented member

Durmaz 1N — medical tech native to Stroyer's Axle

Solomon "Sol" Shrive — member and Allard's friend

Natalie Drouin — former maid to Scott Shaughnessy

Graham Tsoukalas — deceased; killed by own doppelgänger

Jill Haven — deceased; allegedly killed by Officer Mike Prince

Eddie Barndollar — deceased; allegedly killed by Officer Mike Prince

Hector Ferreira — deceased; killed by Scott Shaughnessy

Doreen — teenage lookout at Port to Stroyer's Axle

Donna — a member

Airika — a member

Chola — member and drummer for the Hairless Werewolves

Portsmouth Porthole

Matt Sunderland — deceased; former managing editor, killed by beings from a wind Port

Eric Kuhn — deceased; former reporter, killed by Benazir Allard

Amelia Jones — reporter

Boston, Massachusetts: ***Federal Bureau of Investigation (FBI) Field Office***

Special Agent Mark Ivanov — one of the Assistant Special Agents in Charge (ASACs); seeks to torture and dissect Benazir Allard for "study"

Special Agent Jacob Harriman — ally to Special Agent Ethan Jeong

Katherine "Kat" Marsters — prisoner; former Portsmouth Supervisory Special Agent (SSA)

Marsters Clone 1 — prisoner and clone of Kat Marsters

Marsters Clone 2 — prisoner and clone of Kat Marsters

GRAHAM'S WORLD / WORLD 72 (Master of Ports: The Avid Worm [fire])

No known sentient inhabitants

UNKNOWN ("STROYER'S AXLE WORLD") (**Master of Ports:** The Bloody Swarm [water])

Stroyer's Axle

Ashmael — the Navigator of Stroyer's Axle

UNKNOWN ("AVARICCIA WORLD") (**Master of Ports:** The Hand That Never Closes [quintessence])

Avariccia (City of Games)

Doxe Ungam — deceased; former Noble Lord, killed by Soldier Lord Chaum

Guhnach — deceased; former Priest Lord of the Five-Petaled Temple, killed self to save Divya Allard and Sol Shrive

Chaum — deceased; former Soldier Lord, killed by the Hand That Never Closes

Uench — Merchant Lord

Gluhnt — deceased; former Peasant Lord, killed by Soldier Lord Chaum

Mauguh — a soldier-caste Avariccian

Galg — a priest-caste Avariccian

A unicorn, a griffin, a giant porcupine, a centipillar, a giant snail, a giant turtle, a dragon, an owl-giraffe, a she-wolf, and a goose with ram horns — racing creatures in the Campo

EARTH$_2$ (Master of Ports: Unknown)

Portsmouth, New Hampshire$_2$

Arreth Ryder — co-coordinating relief efforts; know-it-all

Milly Fragonard$_2$ — co-coordinating relief efforts; blocker

Divya Allard$_2$ — presumed dead

Jack Wegman — a homeless man; heartburner

Gaff Briard — Arreth's boyfriend

Solomon "Sol" Shrive$_2$ — injured

Deah Sloane$_2$ — helping with relief efforts

Pete — standing guard during relief efforts

Command Master Chief Brooks — acting head of the Portsmouth Naval Shipyard$_2$; heartburner

A "mindfucker" sailor

Major Wade — acting head of the Pease Air Force Base$_2$

Hampton, New Hampshire$_2$

Father Theo LaPlante$_2$ — preacher for the New Church of Fath

Roderick Lord — a teenage disciple

DRAMATIS PERSONAE

Salaam, Massachusetts

"Mother" Tucker — de facto leader of the Wisewomen boat colony

Elthaba — a healer

Elliott — a healer

Boston, Massachusetts[2]

Dae-seong Jeong — Conductor of the Emerson Corps (mindfuckers)

Phalth — Conductor of the Longfellow Corps (know-it-alls)

Ropha — Conductor of Holmes Corps Black (creeps)

ACKNOWLEDGMENTS

Thanks so much to Kerry Doherty, Abree Murch, Kali Moulton, and Kate Rocheleau for all their help reviewing chapters of this book in our speculative fiction critique group. This book is dedicated to them. Thank you to my writing session companion, Cassie Gustafson (an excellent writer herself—keep an eye out for her work!), and to the Tuesday gang at the Works.

Thanks to Damonza for another amazing book cover, and to Marcelo Gallegos, Bryan Thompson, and Kali Moulton for providing illustrations of the five Port masters in The Shadow Over Portsmouth mythos.

Much of this story was written and revised at the following New Hampshire cafes: Adelle's Coffeehouse in Dover, Cup of Joe and the Portsmouth Book & Bar in Portsmouth, and the Works in Durham. Jo at Cup of Joe has been especially supportive of this series... I'm so grateful! I'm also grateful for the support from the Portsmouth Writers' Night Out community that meets monthly at the Portsmouth Book & Bar.

Portsmouth's Market Square Day takes place on the

second Saturday in June each year. Don't believe everything you read. Do visit the Portsmouth Athenaeum; it's free and open to the public on certain days of the week.

Also, I've moved the FBI Boston Field Office from its actual location outside Boston into the city proper. And neither the Portsmouth city council nor the police department are actually the center of nefarious conspiracies, as far as I know. On the contrary, former and current members of the PD have been quite helpful in my research.

Milly's echolocation helmet is a fine example of something I thought would be cool to exist and then turned out to exist after all. So I swiped a few details from the "Sonic Eye," developed by scientist Jascha Sohl-Dickstein. And I must credit J. Dennis Robinson and his website Seacoast-NH.com for details about the Nazi U-boats in Portsmouth.

The real Salem, Massachusetts, was originally named for the Hebrew word "shalom," but I swapped in the equivalent Arabic word "salaam" for its name in Earth$_2$. Both mean "peace." However, the crescent motif associated with Fath/Breath of the Abyss is not intended to evoke Islam or any other real-world religion.

Thank you to my wife, Jane, for believing in this series. Thanks to Tom, Ginny, Mom, Mary, and the rest of the family for supporting these books and spreading the word. And thanks again to Portsmouth itself—and to Boston in this volume, too. We may never know which type of "notions" it was really nicknamed for, but I have my suspicions.

— Jeff Deck, South Berwick, Maine, July 23, 2019

LIKED THIS BOOK?

Sign up for e-mail updates at www.jeffdeck.com and you'll receive *Tales of the Shadow Over Portsmouth,* a FREE companion book to this series!

And be sure to check out my other titles!

THE PSEUDO-CHRONICLES OF MARK HUNTLEY

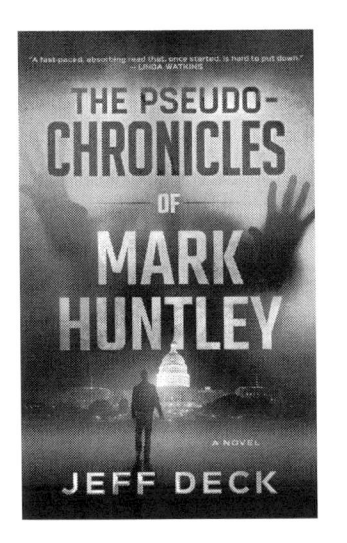

"Deck's writing is seamless and so natural that, as you become immersed in Huntley's increasingly bizarre world, you forget that the story is fiction. This is the mark of a truly gifted writer."
— Linda Watkins, author of the award-winning *Mateguas Island* series

MY NAME IS MARK HUNTLEY. All I really wanted to do was drink cheap beer and blog about my dead-end life. Then I stumbled across a secret war between two sinister alien forces. If I try to stop the war, I may get my friends and loved ones killed. If I don't try, the human race is toast. Oh yeah, and a demonic weapon inside me is probably driving me insane.

If I'm already dead when you find this, you need to carry on the fight.

The Pseudo-Chronicles of Mark Huntley is a blog mutated into a supernatural thriller. If you like the pulse-pounding terror of Stephen King and the smart, funny first-person storytelling of *The Martian*, you'll love meeting Mark Huntley. Find The Pseudo-Chronicles of Mark Huntley online, or request it at your favorite bookstore.

PLAYER CHOICE: AETHER GAMES, BOOK 1

"Master game designer Glen Cullather is having the worst day of his life. Tough luck for him but great news for readers of PLAYER CHOICE. Its twisty plot and high-stakes action will thrill adventure fans, while its reality bending and speculation about the future of privacy will please admirers of the great Philip K. Dick. Check it out: Jeff Deck has got his game on." — James Patrick Kelly, winner of the Hugo, Nebula, and Locus awards

Player Choice is a fast-paced gaming sci-fi adventure that asks: What happens when unreality becomes our reality?

It's 2040. With neural implants, people can play games

in an immersive virtual reality known as the aether space. Game designer Glen Cullather has a plan for the most ambitious aether game ever imagined: a fantasy epic that gives players the freedom to do anything.

But Glen's own life is fragmenting into alternate realities. He can't tell whether his aether game idea has succeeded, or failed miserably. And Freya Janoske is either his biggest rival, or his most intimate partner. Glen must figure out what's real and what's, well, fantasy -- for his own survival! Find the e-book of Player Choice online. Print version coming soon.

ABOUT THE AUTHOR

Jeff Deck is an indie author who lives in Maine with his wife, Jane, and their silly dog, Burleigh. Deck writes science fiction, fantasy, horror, dark fantasy, and other speculative fiction.

Besides *The Shadow Over Portsmouth* series, Deck is the author of the supernatural thriller novel in blog format, *The Pseudo-Chronicles of Mark Huntley,* and the sci-fi gaming adventure novel *Player Choice.* He is also the author, with Benjamin D. Herson, of the nonfiction book *The Great Typo Hunt: Two Friends Changing the World, One Correction at a Time* (Crown/Random House). Deck is also a fiction ghostwriter and editor. He has worked with many authors to help them tell their own stories, and he has contributed content to a couple of video games.

In 2008, Deck took a road trip across the U.S. with friends to fix typos in signage and nearly wound up in federal prison. He enjoys reading speculative fiction, exploring New England with his family, playing video games, and plundering from the past and future.

facebook.com/jeffdeck
twitter.com/tealjeffdeck
instagram.com/jeffdeck

Made in the USA
Middletown, DE
24 July 2019